THE COXEMAN'S MISSION WAS TO PENETRATE THE ENEMY

But the nine nymphs, part of the scientific laboratory, were determined to make it as hard as possible for him.

Rod was a man of action and he could not allow anything to stop him from reaching the power-mad scientist whose twisted mind confused sex with the ability to rule the world. While his co-workers developed The Bomb, he entertained himself with the most unusual harem ever devised by man.

Trapped in a love cycle that could finish him, Rod knows he must not lower his guard for a moment. Somehow he must discover and defuse the bomb or nobody would remain alive in a climax that would be the biggest bang in history.

COXEMAN #5

IT'S GETTING HARDER ALL THE TIME

AN ADULT NOVEL BY BY TROY CONWAY

POPULAR LIBRARY

Copyright © 1968 by Paperback Library Inc.

Popular Library
Hachette Book Group USA
237 Park Avenue
New York, NY 10017

Popular Library is an imprint of Grand Central Publishing. The Popular Library name and logo is a trademark of Hachette Book Group USA, Inc. The Coxeman name and logo is a trademark of Hachette Book Group USA, Inc.

Visit our Web site at www.HachetteBookGroupUSA.com

First Printing: July 1968

Printed in the United States of America

Conway, Troy
It's Getting Harder All the Time / Troy Conway
(Coxeman, #5)

ISBN 0-446-54312-8 / 978-0-446-54312-5

CHAPTER ONE

They were succulently soft, fantastically firm and gorgeously golden. They were high and proud, radiant and round, cuddlesome and caressable. They were, in a word, exquisite—as exquisite and inviting as breasts can be.

And they were mine to do with as I wished—all four of them.

My eyes pored appreciatively over the shimmering expanse of their loveliness. Then my palms closed over the pair on the sides while my face burrowed eagerly between the two in the middle. My tongue traced playful patterns over the captivating curves of one. My neck rubbed rapturously against the bewitching beauty of the other.

A duet of soft, sensuous purrs told me that I was doing exactly what my plural paramours wanted, but for the moment I was less interested in what they wanted than in what was wanted by the third doll in the room—a small, sloe-eyed, stern-faced but still super-sexy bundle of loveliness named Lin Saong.

She sat fully clothed in a chair alongside the bed where my playmates and I were frolicking. Her soft, brown, almond-shaped eyes were scrutinizing us carefully. In one hand she held a cup of tea. In the other she held a snub-nosed forty-five automatic, leveled at my head.

"You needn't spend too much time in those activities which you Occidentals refer to as 'foreplay,' Dr. Damon," she said quietly. "We Orientals believe that the female's sole purpose in the sex act is to accommodate the male."

"As a sex expert, Madame Saong," I replied, momentarily taking my lips from the quivering nipple of the golden-skinned cutie on my right, "I can assure you that

5

foreplay is essential to successful sexual union, whether Oriental or Occidental."

"I'm not interested in successful sexual union, Doctor," she said curtly. "I'm interested in determining whether you are in fact the sex expert which you claim to be." She gestured impatiently with her forty-five. "Now, please proceed."

I promptly went to work south of the border. My facile fingers found their way along two creamy valleys of satin-smooth flesh, then came to rest between two pairs of tantalizing thighs.

The thighs parted invitingly as I neared their apex. At the same time, two slender hands closed around the ramrod-rigid proof of my virility and two others hungrily groped at the cleft between my buttocks.

"Mmmmmm," murmured a velvety voice at my left.

"Mmmmmm," echoed another on my right.

"We're wasting time, Doctor," prodded pistol-packing Lin Saong. "Please be so kind as to—in the American idiom—get the show on the road."

The "show," as she called it, was one of the many three-person sex positions described in the classic Japanese love manuel, *Hikatsu-sho*, or "Book of Secrets." To prove to Lin Saong that I was a bona-fide sex expert and not just some impostor, I had to demonstrate three of the positions in the book. According to our arrangement, she would identify the position I was to demonstrate only by telling me the name it was given in the book. For example, "Position of the Mysterious Pearl and the Two Crabs." Then, without consulting the text, I had to assume the position with the twin playmates she had supplied for the demonstration.

But there was more to the positions of *Hikatsu-sho* than mere sexual gymnastics. The anonymous author of that venerable Japanese erotic classic had stated explicitly that each party in the sex act must achieve orgasm—and all at the same time. I reminded Lin Saong of this, and I said, "Without adequate foreplay, our little show is going to—in the American idiom—lay a big fat egg."

She unscrambled the mixed metaphors and her brow fur-

6

rowed. I could see that she wasn't quite prepared for the last curve I threw her.

The reason for her unpreparedness was simple. Lin Saong wasn't Japanese. She was Chinese. More precisely, she was Communist Chinese. After Mao and his bully boys overthrew the Nationalist government in 1949, every erotic book on the Chinese mainland was destroyed. Consequently a whole generation had grown to maturity without being aware of the sexual practices and sexual literature of China's Golden Age.

Now, Lin Saong, as a member of Red China's new generation—and, incidentally, as a member of CHILLER, the Red Chinese all-female espionage agency—had come to test my erotic expertise. Since she had no genuine Chinese erotic works to use as a model for the test, she had had to borrow from the erotic lore of Japan. But she evidently hadn't read the entire book that she planned to test me on.

"Well," she said blushingly after a moment, "use foreplay if you must. But please be quick about it. Remember that while we dally here an enemy of both your country and mine is perfecting a bomb that could be as formidable as any weapon either of our countries has in its arsenal. Every minute counts."

"If you're in such a hurry," I shot back, "why don't you just dispense with the test?"

She hesitated for a moment, as if giving the suggestion serious consideration. Then, smiling slightly, she reasserted her old authority. "Unless you prove beyond a doubt that you're the expert my agency has told you are, I can't risk sharing with you the information we've acquired."

I could've debated with her. I could've argued, for example, that the United States wouldn't have sent me on this mission unless I were the sex expert whom everybody seemed to agree was the only person who could do the job. Or I could've pointed out that she herself evidently knew so little about sex that no matter what I did with the two girls, she'd really have no way of knowing whether I was a sex expert or not.

But I didn't feel like arguing. And I did feel like getting

7

back to the project at hand, namely what *Hikatsu-sho* described as "Position of The Mysterious Pearl and The Two Crabs." Reimmersing my face in the twin cushions formed by my dual lovelies' breasts, I murmured, "Okay, Madame Saong, the show will go on." Then I brought my fingers back into play against the delicate folds of my playmates' most sensitive parts.

Twin purrs of delight told me that my golden-skinned partners were glad I was getting down to business. As a matter of fact, judging from the way the gals began writhing and moaning. I was the best thing that had happened to them since the day they discovered that boys and girls are truly different. Obviously nearly twenty years of Mao's anti-sex propaganda hadn't extinguished their natural urge to merge.

And they weren't exactly the worst thing that had happened to me either. It's not every day that a guy finds himself in bed with a delicious duo like these dolls—even if the guy is the world's foremost authority on sex.

Their soft, smooth bodies, pressing lovingly against my arms and chest, set off hot sparks of passion deep inside me. The gentle, undulating movements of their hips worked hard at fanning the sparks into flame. The slow, provocative caresses of their slender hands on my excited manhood let me know that when the flame came it would be one hell of a conflagration.

I probed deeper and deeper into the love-starved recesses between their thighs. In reply, the twin cuties began writhing all the more passionately. The doll at my right found my neck with her lips and nibbled on it fiercely. The one on my left brought her tender-lipped mouth to my ear, and while teasingly tonguing the lobe, whispered something in Chinese. I don't understand the language, but it didn't take too much imagination to realize what she was telling me: she was raring to go.

Frankly, so was I. But before I went I wanted to make sure that my tantalizing twosome were heated up like they'd never been heated up before. I knew that in the days ahead I'd need all the help I could get from the girls from CHILLER. The best way to insure that I'd get it was to make them so hungry for my loving that they could never have enough of it.

My fingers continued to search out the depths of the delectable caverns which Chinese poets of centuries past have described variously as The Jade Treasure, The Dark Vale, The Heart of the Flower, The Jewel Terrace and The Jade Gate. Each of my movements sent new ripples of excitement through my passion-drenched playmates' quivering bodies. "Ooooooohhhhhhh," cooed the one at my left. And the one on my right murmured something in Chinese that sounded very much like, "Now!"

But I still wasn't ready for the grand finale. Abandoning my nestling place between the dolls' breasts, I kissed my way up one girl's throat. Then, after kissing her lightly on the lips, I passionately kissed the other girl. Next I kissed the first girl again, then the second and alternated again and again. The boiling point was getting near.

With each kiss I maneuvered their faces closer and closer together. Finally the three of our faces were pressed against each other and I was kissing both girls at once. My tongue darted hungrily through one set of lips, then the other. At the same time, the girls' fiery tongues hungrily probed my mouth.

Now the twin cuties were really raring to go. Their steel-taut bodies were arched up off the bed. Their hips were pumping away furiously. Their hands clutched at my manhood as if it was The Staff of Life.

From somewhere behind me I could hear the sensuous panting of a third girl—none other than CHILLER-Chief Lin Saong. It occurred to me that more than five minutes had passed without her saying a single word about cutting short the foreplay. Evidently she was getting her kicks out of the proceedings too.

But I didn't spend too much time thinking about Lin Saong. My dynamic duo was all fired up and so was I. Hoisting myself up on my hands and knees, I began silently maneuvering the twin cuties into place for The Position of the Mysterious Pearl and the Two Crabs.

The position drew its name from the Oriental euphemisms for the sex organs and the bodily postures involved. A rather free translation of the instructions in *Hikatsu-sho* reads something like this:

"Girl Number One kneels before the man, her legs spread wide, her buttocks high in the air and her shoulders flush against the bed. The man crouches over her, entering her from behind in the manner of coitus practiced among beasts. Girl Number Two then lies across Girl Number One's back, her head being in the same direction as the head of Girl Number One, her legs being draped over the man's shoulders. The man then brings his mouth to her Mysterious Pearl and proceeds to polish it with his tongue at the same time that he assaults the Jade Gate of Girl Number One with his Lotus Stalk."

In other words, I was supposed to make it, doggie-style, with Girl Number One at the same time that I went down on Girl Number Two, and according to the part of the book which Lin Saong evidently never got around to reading, all three of us were supposed to have orgasm at the same time.

Girl Number One obediently slipped into position as I guided her with my hands. She might not have read *Hikatsu-sho*, but she certainly was no stranger to making it doggie-style. Once I had urged her body into a kneeling position in front of me, her legs parted automatically and her buttocks instinctively rose high into the air. Then I maneuvered my "lotus stalk" into place between them, and she hungrily shimmied against me, immersing the weapon to the hilt. A quiver of delight shook her entire body as I hit bottom, and her hips promptly took up a slow gyrating movement.

Girl Number Two didn't get the message quite so quickly. I tried to ease her into place atop Girl Number One's back, but she didn't seem to understand what I had in mind. If anything, she seemed a little teed off at me —probably because I had made a play for Girl Number One before I made my play for her.

I thought of asking Lin Saong to translate into Chinese exactly what I wanted done, but I finally decided that it'd be more fun setting the thing up strictly via nonverbal communication. Taking the miffed cutie's face in my hands, I

10

kissed her gently on the lips. Then I slowly began kissing my way down her body.

By the time I reached her bellybutton, she had a pretty good indication that I didn't plan to stop there, and she suddenly wasn't miffed anymore. After that it was just a case of guiding her into position and maneuvering her legs over my shoulders. I kissed my way down her smooth golden thighs, which parted obligingly as I neared their zenith. Then my tongue gently invaded the tender folds of her womanhood, and The Mysterious Pearl wasn't a mystery any longer.

Girl Number One began gyrating her hips more quickly. The searing heat of her boiling passion-pit sent electric tongues of sensation coarsing through my entire body. I thrust harder, and she responded by gyrating all the more furiously. Her frantic movements told me that she was very close to the proverbial edge of the ledge, which suited me fine, because so was I.

And so was Girl Number Two. As my tongue flickered hotly over the satin-smooth slickness of her Mysterious Pearl, her thighs scissored wildly around my face and her feet pounded fiercely against my back. Her hips skittered madly back and forth, and her trim, flat belly began heaving.

"Ahhhhhhh!" she sighed, or the Chinese equivalent thereof. Then her clenched fists began pounding against the bed in a gesture that needed no translation: she wasn't merely at the edge of the ledge, she was off it and sky-rocketing up, up and away into the orgasmic stratosphere.

Determined to observe the letter as well as the spirit of the law set down in *Hikatsu-sho*, I hammered all the harder against the furiously gyrating buttocks of Girl Number One. The first few strokes made her moan. The next few made her groan. And the few after that set off the ecstatic explosion which the boys on Madison Avenue might describe as The Big O. Like Girl Number Two, she was up, up and away—but really AWAY!

And not a second too soon, because I was right there with her. In a mad moment of supreme bliss, my body

11

erupted into spasm after spasm of overwhelming delight.

For all of a minute neither of us said anything. Our bodies remained in place like three statues in a display of erotic sculpture. The only sound in the room was the cacophonous symphony of our deep breathing. Then, slowly and gently, I eased the legs of Girl Number Two over my head and onto the bed, and disengaged myself from the still quivering Dark Vale of Girl Number One.

"Well," I said to Lin Saong, "so much for the first position. Now what would you like for an encore."

My gun-wielding examiner looked at me through glazed eyes. Her expression told me that she was nothing less than awe-struck at the performance. I naturally hadn't paid much attention to her while I was going through my paces, but it was obvious that she had paid a lot of attention to me—and it was equally obvious that the spectacle had moved her. Her tea cup had somehow or other found its way onto a night table, and her arms were draped lifelessly across her legs, the snub-nosed forty-five automatic dangling impotently between her knees. "Dr. Damon," she said quietly, "you really know your business."

I flashed a self-satisfied smile. "Like I said, Madame Saong, I'm an expert. Now what's the next test you've devised?"

Her soft, almond-shaped eyes did a quick tour of my body. "I—I—" she began. Then she let the sentence trail off.

I quickly filled the conversation gap. "May I suggest that you participate personally in the next exercise? After all, *Hikatsu-sho* says that all parties in the sex act must experience orgasm simultaneously, and the only way you have of knowing that the girls did experience it is to take their word for it. If you want to be sure that I'm a sex expert, the best way to find out is to try me yourself."

She hesitated for a moment. Then her expression of awe slowly gave way to a stern, businesslike look. "That won't be necessary, Doctor," she said. "I've seen all I have to see."

"But you can't really be sure that I'm an expert," I argued. "You'll never really know unless you try me your-

12

self." I wasn't being magnamimous, and I wasn't being sarcastic. There was something about the cool, unruffled demeanor of my super-aloof captor that turned me on. As a matter of fact, I wanted to make love to her even more than I wanted to do an encore with the two cuties on the bed.

But Lin Saong wasn't buying. "Sex, Doctor," she said dryly, "is a bourgeois capitalist pursuit, an activity which drains the energies of those who participate in it and which serves no end other than that of base, sensory gratification. My assistants have no choice but to lend themselves to this degrading experience because our mission demands it. But I, more highly placed in our organization than they, need not suffer the same degradation." She gestured with her pistol. "You may put on your clothes now."

"But," I protested, "I've only demonstrated one of the positions from *Hikatsu-sho*. You said you wanted me to demonstrate three."

She smiled sardonically. "I realize that it would gratify your debauched capitalistic nature to degrade these poor girls even further, but having seen your demonstration, I'm now fully convinced that you're the sex expert you claim to be. No one but a libertine of the lowest order could lend himself so unabashedly to a contempuous exercise of the sort which I've just observed." She gestured again with the pistol. "The test is over, Doctor, and you've passed it with—in the American idiom—flying colors. Now get dressed."

"But," I argued lamely, "I might be part of an anti-Chinese plot. I might be someone the United States sent here to further complicate your attempts to foil the plans of your enemies. Surely you ought to test me further."

Her smile broadened into a full-blown grin. "You're legitimate, Damon," she said softly. "Your eagerness to continue these horrible activities testifies to your legitimacy even more than your expertise does." She barked something in Chinese to the two girls, then turned back to me. "Now get dressed. We've got some business to attend to."

I could see that there was no point in trying to force the issue. Disappointed at having expertised myself out of two more groovy sexcapades, and even more disappointed at having failed to lure Lin Saong into participating in one or both of them, I slowly began dressing. My twin playmates did likewise.

Lin Saong polished off the remains of her cup of tea and smiled at me benignly. "And now, Doctor," she said, "we're ready to begin our collaborative effort against our countries' mutual enemy. Tomorrow morning I shall telephone my contact at the Belgravian harem. I shall instruct her to pave the way for your arrival. Once she has laid the necessary groundwork, you'll be welcomed at the harem and you'll be given the opportunity to demonstrate what a sex expert you really are. The fate of both our countries—indeed the fate of the entire world—rests on the success of your demonstration."

I was listening with only one ear. The peptalk Lin Saong was giving me wasn't much different from the one I'd received before leaving the States. So, pulling on my T-shirt, I let her prattle on, while the greater part of my attention focused on the twin cuties who a few minutes earlier had been my sexmates.

They were sitting side by side on the edge of the bed, their small, pert breasts jutting up provocatively from beneath the fine fabric of their gauze-thin tunics, their smooth and slender legs stretched enticingly before them. I imagined myself parting those slender legs and launching another exercise of the sort which poetic Chinese writers of ages past might describe as an invasion of the Hidden Gully by Great General Lotus Stalk.

"No doubt," Lin Saong went on, "your superiors in America have briefed you on the dangers which lurk ahead, dangers to you personally as well as to my contact in the Belgravian harem. It is imperative, therefore, that you conduct yourself with absolute discretion. Should our mutual enemy acquire even the slightest suspicion that you're aware of his murderous plan, your life won't be worth—in the American idiom—a plugged nickel. And of course, if you fail to obtain the information we require, the results will be disastrous for all concerned."

My focus shifted from the bodies of the twin cuties to the body of Lin Saong. As she spoke, she leaned forward in her chair. Her bountiful, uncorseted breasts—unusually large for an Oriental girl—jiggled invitingly against the contours of her loose-fitting hopsack blouse like a pair of grapefruits in a burlap sack. My well-trained eyes made out the outlines of her firm, upthrust nipples, then traversed the marvelous expanse of her sensuous, slacks-encased thighs.

"Tomorrow evening," she continued, "you'll be invited to the Belgravian harem, thanks to my contact there, and you'll be introduced to all the people whose help you'll need to accomplish the mission. If you employ your talents wisely, you should be able to learn from these people the exact location of the bomb which our enemy is now developing. Once you find out where the bomb is, you're to relay the information to me via radio. I'll supply you with a miniature transmitter and everything else you'll need. You'll get these things before you leave."

She shifted in her seat, and her long legs swung to one side. My eyes zeroed in on the succulent curves of her hips, which strained maddeningly against the tightness of her slacks.

"Once I've been informed of the location of the bomb," she went on, "I'll relay the message to headquarters of PUF, the Belgravian Peoples' United Front, which opposes the regime whose development of the bomb has proved to be a threat to both your government and mine. Aided by technicians whom we have supplied, and, of course, using weapons which we have provided, PUF with attack the outpost where the bomb is stored and will dismantle it, or, failing that, destroy it."

I bolted upright in my seat. Suddenly I had lost all interest in the sexual endowments of both Lin Saong and her two cuddlesome subordinates.

"I was told back in the United States," I said, fumbling with my socks, "that you'd relay the information to the United Nations, which would send a peace mission to demand that Belgravia voluntarily surrender the bomb."

She smiled. "That was the original plan. Unfortunately

15

my superiors have since decided that an alternate plan must be put into effect. We will now follow the alternate plan."

"But," I protested, "if PUF fails to dismantle the bomb—if, as you put it, the bomb is 'destroyed,' hundreds of thousands of people, even millions of people, might be killed. My country never agreed to an arrangment like that!"

"Your country," she said softly, "agreed that Dr. Rod Damon would undertake this mission as a subordinate to my country's *chargé d'affaires*—namely, me, I'm telling you, Damon, that we're going to follow the alternate plan. Your job is not to wonder why; your job is to do or die."

I gulped. Actually the change of plan didn't take me completely by surprise. Before leaving the states, I'd known that CHILLER might try something funny. And steps had been taken to insure that my team would stay one up on their team. Accompanying me to Belgravia was a United States radio expert whose only job would be to intercept the messages I radioed to Lin Saong and to relay them back to the States.

But how could I tip off my contact to the change in plans without arousing Lin Saong's suspicions? And even if I could tip him off, would the United States be able to take action to prevent CHILLER from carrying out its alternate plan?

"One thing more, Damon," said Lin Saong. "My superiors have concluded that the Belgravian bomb should be completely developed within two weeks. It is your job to pinpoint its location before the two weeks are up. If you fail, there will be no choice for my country but to support PUF in a full-scale assault on Belgravia. We will supply PUF with airplanes, bombs, artillery pieces and all other necessary weapons. Naturally the assault will explode the bomb, killing everyone in Belgravia—including yourself."

I gulped again. With each sentence she uttered, the stakes of the game were getting higher. I finished buttoning my shirt, then stepped into my trousers. As I did, I heard a small voice inside me ask, "Damon, you idiot, how could you ever let yourself get into a mess like this?"

"Ah yes, Damon," Lin Saong added, "still one more thing. When you arrived in Belgravia today, you were accompanied by another American. Our organization has identified him as a United States agent, a radio specialist, whose job presumably is to intercept your messages to me and to relay them back to the United States. Since it was my country's agreement with your country that you would be working with us alone and unaided, we have taken the liberty of rendering him useless to you. In other words, he's been killed." She took a leather case from the night table drawer and tossed it onto the bed. "This wallet contains his identification papers. If you come out of this mission alive, I'd suggest you return them to his next of kin back in America."

I did a triple gulp. When I came to Belgravia, I was counting on the radio specialist as my only link with the home team. Now my link was gone. I tugged my trousers over my hips.

"Finish dressing," said Lin Saong, "and I'll have you taken back to your own room. The car which will bring you · to the harem will be ready at seven in the morning. That's only six hours away. Meanwhile I'd advise that you get all the sleep you can. You'll need it."

I zipped up my pants.

She wasn't kidding when she said I'd need some sleep. Judging from what I'd been told to expect at the harem, I'd have to be as well-rested as rested could be.

But sleep wasn't all I needed.

What I needed even more was an out.

And I'd be damned if I could think of one.

The small voice inside me boomed out loud and clear, "Damon, Damon, Damon, how the *hell* did you ever get into a mess like this?"

17

CHAPTER TWO

How *did* I get into a mess like this?

It all started, believe it or not, with a classified ad in *The New York Times*: "HELP WANTED, virile male to assist in sexual experiments, Belgravia, Africa. Salary: $1,000 per week. All relocation expenses paid. Apply in person, Madame Champville, Belgravian Embassy, Washington, D.C."

I didn't answer the ad. In fact, I didn't even see it. I was playing spy-versus-spy in Rome when it appeared, and frankly I wouldn't have answered it even if I had seen it.

True, I'm a virile male—in fact, an insatiably virile male. I'm afflicted (or blessed, if you prefer) with a condition called "priapism." In every case other than mine known to medical science, priapists experience perpetual penile erection but are unable to achieve orgasm. Thanks to an unexplainable biological quirk, I enjoy the best of both worlds; I'm not only always ready to go, but I invariably have one hell of a good time when I get there.

Also true, a grand a week isn't exactly chicken feed. It's five times as much money as I ordinarily make, and in Belgravia, Africa, most of it would be tax free.

But Belgravia, Africa, was the last place in the world I'd choose to demonstrate my insatiable virility—even if the grand a week was tax free and even if all relocation expenses were paid. Call it patriotism if you like, or call it a homing instinct, but the fact is that I liked staying in the good old U.S.A.

Unfortunately a certain guy who's in the employ of the U.S. government—a guy with a shaggy, walrus-like moustache and a nasty sense of humor, a guy who likes sending me off on spy hunts to all four corners of the globe—did see the ad. And, in a manner of speaking, he answered it for me. The result was that I now found myself facing death on one side, treason on another, and a jail sentence on the third.

If you find this confusing, don't feel bad. I find it even more confusing than you do, but as my pal with the walrus moustache likes to say, that's the way the cookie crumbles. Or in another of his devastatingly witty phrases, if you can't stand the heat, stay out of the kitchen. And since I was already in the kitchen, there was no choice but to stand the heat.

Maybe I'd better spell things out a bit more explicitly.

My name, as you no doubt have gathered, is Damon. Rod Damon. More precisely, Dr. Rod Damon.

I hold a legitimate Ph.D. in sociology, and I'm an associate professor at a major university in the northeastern United States. Also I'm founder, director and chief beneficiary of the League for Sexual Dynamics.

The "League" is more of a pleasure than a business, although for me it accomplishes both purposes at the same time. It's something I cooked up in my pre-doctoral days, when I was a sex-happy young student trying to figure out a way to both have my sociological cake and eat it too. I applied for grants from knowledge-hungry research foundations and used the money to study the sexual mores of various segments of contemporary society. My findings are published in all the major journals, earning me a reputation as one of the country's most distinguished behavioral scientists, and my field studies led to my bedding down with some of the grooviest chicks ever hatched.

My first project was a study of the sexual behavior of American coeds. My next was a study of parallels between the sexual behavior of American coeds and contemporary non-college females. Subsequently I studied the sexual behavior of female graduate students, of female Ph.D.'s, of female college dropouts, of female college kick-outs, of suburban housewives, of urban housewives, of rural housewives, of New York career girls, of Los Angeles

19

career girls, of Washington (D.C.) career girls, of London career girls, of Paris career girls and of Rome career girls.

Somewhere along the line, my studies came to the attention of the Thaddeus X. Coxe Foundation, an ostensibly right wing front-group but a cover for the United States' most secretive espionage agency. And one night while I was playing research games with one of my students, I was interrupted by two hoods from this agency, who promptly brought me to their boss, the aforementioned guy with the walrus moustache.

Walrus-moustache had learned of a plot by a group of Neo-Nazis, based in Hamburg, Germany, to lure the United States, Russia and China into World War III. He also had learned of a certain very-mature-looking sixteen-year-old who had participated in one of my research projects. Since carnal knowledge of a person younger than eighteen is, in my state, statutory rape, punishable by twenty years imprisonment, I had two choices: (1) go to jail, or (2) become a Coxeman and spy on the Neo-Nazis. I chose to become a Coxeman and we stopped the war before it ever got started.

A short while later, when I was researching the sex behavior of America's hippies, Walrus-moustache uncovered a bizarre plot to take over the United States by polluting the Potomac River with L.S.D. and staging a military coup while Washington, D.C., was freaked-out on the trip to end all trips. I was tapped to foil that plot also and again saved America from a fate nothing short of disastrous.

By this time, I was sure, I had dispatched Uncle Sam's enemies once and for all. But I'd been wrong. In short order, Walrus-moustache also called on me to foil the plot by two mad Italian scientists to breed a computer-sired race of antisocial superpeople and then the plot of another group of whackpots to take over the world by scientifically lowering temperatures far below the livable level all over the globe.

Then, back on campus a few months later—and totally engrossed in my latest sexual research project—I was visited by Walrus-moustache again. He dragged me out of

20

a warm bed and an even warmer girl's arms to tell me that the Free World faced a greater menace than ever before.

"We're really in trouble this time, Damon," he said, his voice quavering dramatically. "We stand poised on the brink of all-out, multi-nation nuclear war. Unless we act fast, and efficiently, the whole globe may go up in a mushroom cloud."

I replied with my typical enthusiasm. "Can't it wait until next week? I just met this groovy blonde, and I'd really like some time to get to know her better."

He played the same trump card he had played to lure me into all my other capers as a Coxeman—the threat of a jail sentence.

"Remember," he reminded me, "statutory rape isn't the only crime we can prove that you've committed. There's that possession-of-narcotics charge you were booked on in New York while you were working on a case. There's a matter of unlawful entry into the United States—in case you hadn't noticed, your passport expired while you were in Rome handling a case. There's also an unnatural-crimes-against-nature rap we can pin on you. And there are all of a dozen other charges we could come up with if we really put our minds to it."

I muttered a word the letters of which consisted of the initials in the phrase which described the first crime on the list—For Unlawful Carnal Knowledge. Then I told him what he wanted to hear. "Okay, deal me in. Now what's this new caper all about?"

He smiled, obviously satisfied with the speed with which I had capitulated. Then his smile vanished, and a worried look furrowed his brow. "Damon," he said solemnly, "a bomb is now being built which makes the atom bomb and the hydrogen bomb look in comparison like a couple of Fourth of July firecrackers—a bomb which, in one fell swoop, can wipe out the entire Northern Hemisphere. According to our calculations, it'll take no more than two or three months for the bomb to be completed. When that happens, we'll be at the mercy of the country that's perfected it. And judging from what we've seen so far, the country is absolutely merciless."

21

My eyebrows arched quizzically. "What country are we talking about? Red China?"

He shook his head. "No, they're as worried about it as we are."

My eyebrows inched higher. "Then who? Russia?"

"No. They're in the same boat as us and Red China."

"Then who? Surely not France."

"No. DeGaulle has given us more than a fair share of troubles lately, but this isn't one of them."

"Then who?"

He chuckled mirthlessly. "That's the question which, until three weeks ago, has had all of us—Russia, China, France and the United States—going around in circles. Finally, out of desperation, all four nations pooled their resources, and now, thanks to Red China, we've come up with a candidate. The United States is counting on you to get that candidate elected—or rejected."

I scratched my head. "If you're trying to confuse me, you're doing a damned good job of it."

He smiled. "Well, let me start at the beginning. Then maybe the whole thing'll make sense."

I smiled back—bitterly. "I'm waiting."

He leaned forward in his chair, and his eyes took on a far-away look. "On February first," he began, "U.S. monitors detected a 'clean' hydrogen bomb blast in the south Atlantic. The explosion was above-ground, which violated the nuclear test ban treaty of nineteen sixty-two. So naturally we checked with the other signatories of the treaty—Russia, Britian and France—to see if it was their bomb. All three insisted that it wasn't, and after all the evidence was weighed, we became convinced that they were telling the truth. The finger of suspicion then pointed at the only other nuclear power, Red China. But evidently Red China was as much in the dark about the blast as we were, because Mao, through his embassy in Paris, put out feelers to us, Britain, France and Russia. He said, in effect, that if the bomb didn't belong to any of us, he'd be willing to join us in a collaborative mission to find out who it actually did belong to."

22

"And we believed him?"

"Yes. You see, the bomb was sophisticated, but it wasn't as sophisticated as the previous bomb Red China had exploded. This suggested to us that whoever had exploded it was a new nation, a nation which previously did not have nuclear capabilities. Consequently we sent a delegate to an ultra-top-secret, five-power conference at Geneva, designed to determine who actually had exploded the bomb. An investigation was conducted and the conclusion was that our original suspicion had been correct. The country which exploded the bomb was a new nation, a previously nonnuclear nation."

"But which nation?"

"That, dear Damon, was the question. The United States and Britain suspected one of the Communist-bloc countries—perhaps Yugoslavia or Albania. But we had the assurances of Russia and Red China that no Communist-bloc nation had been supported in a nuclear program, and these assurances, all things being considered, were enough to satisfy us. France, meanwhile, believed that a United States-backed country was the culprit—perhaps Australia or Nationalist China. But we were able to prove to everyone's satisfaction that neither of these nations nor any of our other close allies was involved. Russia suspected Israel, and produced evidence that the Israeli do in fact have the nuclear 'secret.' However, the Geneva commission investigation showed that, while Israel might have had the secret, it certainly did not have the money to support advanced testing of the sort which had taken place in the south Atlantic, especially after the six-day war with Nasser and his allies. Finally Red China voiced its suspicions, and the country it named came as such a surprise to all the other nuclear powers that we could scarcely believe Mao and his people weren't joking. But the evidence now in hand suggests that the Red Chinese not only were deadly serious but also were dead right."

"For Pete's sake, which country did they suspect?"

A small smile curled his lips. "Would you believe," he asked, savoring the suspenseful moment, "Belgravia?"

My eyebrows strained upward until they threatened to merge with my hairline. "Belgravia?" I echoed. "Where in hell is Belgravia?"

He chuckled reprovingly. "Evidently you've been too busy with sex research to keep abreast of developments among Africa's so-called emerging nations. Belgravia is a new country in the historical as well as in the nuclear sense. In fact, it's only eight-and-a-half years old. It's one of the five republics which once constituted French Equatorial Africa."

I gulped. "How does a two-bit country like that become a nuclear power?"

His chuckle expanded into a full-blown, bitterly mirthless laugh. "Red China has a theory, and as much as the United States might hate to admit it, the theory makes sense. I'll tell you about the theory in a minute, but first let me cue you in on something of Belgravia's history and current politics."

I leaned back in my seat. "Cue away."

He snapped open a loose-leaf notebook labeled "U.S. Department of State Background Notes" and leafed through the pages. Finally he found the page he wanted and began reading: "Belgravia, covering an area of forty-two thousand square miles, lies just south of the Equator on the west coast of Africa. It is bordered on the north by Gabon, on the east and south by Republic of Congo and on the west by the Atlantic Ocean. Except for its capital, Rodin, and its principal city, Port duBeers, nearly all of the country is covered by dense equatorial rain forest. The climate is hot and humid. From June to September there is virtually no rain but high humidity. In December and January there is occasional rain. During the remaining months rainfall is heavy. At Rodin the annual average rainfall is more than one hundred inches. On the northwest coast it is one hundred and fifty inches."

"It sounds like a great place to live if you happen to be a fish."

"From what I've heard, even the fish don't like it. But of course we're not asking you to live there—only to visit."

24

"Thanks," I murmured dryly. "I'm always grateful for small favors."

Ignoring the comment, he continued reading.

"With only about three hundred and twenty thousand inhabitants, Belgravia is one of the least populated of any of the five republics of former French Equatorial Africa. The capital city of Rodin has a population of about eighteen thousand, and Port duBeers, the principal seaport, has a population of about twenty-two thousand. The remainder of the population is concentrated in villages along rivers and roads, while large areas of the interior lie empty. During the last one hundred years there has been a decline in population because of disease, but increased medical care and social services have recently halted this trend."

"I'm glad to hear that it's been halted," I confessed.

"Don't worry, we'll inoculate you against anything communicable before you go." He dipped back into his notebook and resumed reading. "Almost all the Belgravians are Bantu. There are at least twenty tribal groups with separate languages and cultures. The largest tribe in the Guwai, numbering about sixty thousand. Next largest is the Ogana with twenty thousand. Then are the Keross with eight thousand. The remainder of the population is divided among seventeen other tribes. Tribal boundaries are less sharply drawn than anywhere else in Africa with the possible exception of Gabon. French, the official national language, is a unifying force."

"*Vive l'unité!*" I quipped.

"Belgravia," he went on, not pausing to acknowledge my side-splitting humor, "was first visited by Europeans in the fifteenth century, when Portugese explorers came seeking slaves. Dutch, British, French and Belgian traders followed in the sixteenth century. Belgravia first came under French protection by treaties with the coastal chiefs in 1840, then was ceded to Belgium under a treaty with King Leopold II, signed in 1907. The country achieved independence on June thirtieth, 1960, the same day that the Belgian government granted independence to its better-known African possession, the Congo. Since that time,

Belgravia has been a republic with a presidential form of government. Under the constitution of 1961, it has a unicameral National Assembly of thirty-five members. The Assembly is elected for five years, but may be dismissed by the President if he deems such a dismissal to be in the national interest. The President, who is chief of state and chief of government, is elected for seven years. All other members of the government are appointed by the President, who can also recall any of them."

"And to think," I mused, "that some Americans complain about our president's power."

Walrus-moustache smiled. "Well," he conceded, looking up from his notebook, "the Belgravian presidency is somewhat autocratic. And frankly, the current office-holder, Dr. Albert Douzi, might appear to Western observers as something of a cross between Spain's Generalissimo Franco and the Black Muslims' Elijah Mohammed. But when all is said and done, Dr. Douzi unquestionably commands the support of the vast majority of his constituents."

"How? With machine guns?"

"Not quite. You see, Douzi is a favorite son of the dominant Guwai tribe. His father was chief of the tribe and a very benign leader. Douzi was educated in European schools, got his A.B. and M.A. degrees from Oxford, then his M.D. and Ph.D. degrees from the Sorbonne. He specialized in psychiatry, and was faculty member at the Sorbonne until 1959, when he returned to Belgravia. He was a principal force in the nation's drive for independence and almost single-handedly drew up the present constitution."

"Which explains, no doubt, why the president enjoys virtually unlimited powers."

"Perhaps. In any case, most Belgravians feel that, were it not for Douzi, the country would still be a Belgian colony, and a rather miserable one at that. Before independence, the average per capita income among Belgravians was about three million *guilleux* a year, or roughly forty American dollars. Laborers in the duBeers diamond mines, Belgravia's only significant industry, worked at what were literally starvation wages. Many people lived

26

only by killing what game they could in the rain forests. And as I mentioned earlier, disease was so rampant that the country had a rapidly dwindling population rate—this despite the face that the use of contraceptives was all but unknown. The infant mortality rate was something like a thousand times that of the United States. Douzi's new government changed all that. He nationalized the diamond mines and began paying workers a fair wage. He established medical clinics not only in the cities of Rodin and Port duBeers, but also in the outlying districts. Schools were set up, and parents whose children became students automatically received a generous government subsidy. In short, under Douzi, Belgravia moved in eight and a half years from a poverty-stricken, disease-infested hellhole to a thriving, prosperous independent state. The price which the people of Belgravia paid for this prosperity was that of accepting Douzi's dictatorship. But even under Douzi's autocratic form of government they enjoy more of a say in the management of their own affairs than they did when Belgravia was a Belgian colony. So, any way you slice it, they've come a long way and they're pretty happy with their situation. Or more precisely, they were pretty happy with their situation until PUF started stirring up trouble."

"Puff? As in 'Puff, the Magic Dragon'?"

"No, as in Peoples' United Front. But your 'Magic Dragon' reference is on target, because PUF is a Commie front. More specifically it's a Red Chinese front. The situation is somewhat similar to that in Vietnam, where the so-called National Liberation Front is in action."

"I don't see the parallel. Vietnam's NLF is opposed to the Saigon regime for a number of very good reasons. If Dr. Albert Douzi's government is as benign and socially oriented as you say, exactly what is PUF opposed to?"

He sighed. "It's one of those complex situations, Damon, that make international politics the crazy game that it is. True, Douzi has brought about a lot of reforms. But the PUF people have persuaded a lot of Belgravians that more reforms are called for. According to PUF, Douzi's work has already been done and the time has come for an even more representative democracy than Belgravia

27

now enjoys. Frankly the United States might sympathize with PUF's demands were they made within a constitutional context. But PUF advocates a violent—i.e., military—overthrow of Douzi and his people. It's the old Commie pattern of getting a foot in the door, then a leg, then the whole body. PUF started by demanding that Douzi relinquish the right to dismiss the assembly. The United States, which until recently was quite friendly with Douzi, suggested that he not only do that but that he also institute additional reforms which would bring his government closer to what we like to think of as the democratic ideal. Unfortunately he couldn't see things our way. He responded to the PUF challenge by waging a campaign of military suppression. Press censorship was instituted, and leaders of dissident political groups were jailed. This naturally gave PUF more to harp about and they've been harping incessantly ever since. Douzi, meanwhile, has become more inflexible than ever. The result is that Belgravia today has become almost a police state. From where we sit, Douzi appears determined not to budge one inch, and PUF appears more determined than ever that Douzi must be overthrown. The situation is very explosive. According to U.S. State Department on-the-scene observers, civil war may break out almost any day now. The majority of Belgravians, to be sure, still side with Douzi. But a substantial and ever-growning minority sees things the Commie way."

"Where does the mysterious hydrogen bomb blast fit into this picture?"

"Red China, as I said before, has a theory which links the bomb to Douzi's government, and as much as the United States might hate to admit that Mao and his people are one up on us spy-wise, the theory makes sense."

"What exactly is the theory?"

He leaned back in his seat. Again his eyes took on a faraway look. "About eight months before the hydrogen bomb blast, a classified ad appeared in leading newspapers throughout the world seeking the services of a virile male for mysterious sexual experiments in Belgravia." He slipped an envelope from inside his jacket, extracted a clipping of the ad that had appeared in *The New York Times*, and handed it to me. "About two months after the ad appeared, Belgravia began inviting prominent physicists to lecture at its newly founded National University. The physicists who were invited had three things in common: they were all from Communist-bloc countries, they were all intimately connected with their countries' nuclear development programs, and they were all female. All told, nine such physicists went to Belgravia. None ever returned."

"In other words," I put in, "Red China thinks that Douzi lured the female physicists to Belgravia to give lectures, then enticed them to stay there and work on his nuclear program by offering them the services of the virile male he had hired through his classified ads."

"Precisely. And as I said, the theory makes a lot of sense. As everyone knows, sex behind the Iron Curtain is very much a forbidden thing. It's not hard to imagine how frustrated the nine female physicists might have become in their antisexual Communist homelands. Douzi could have helped this sexual hunger along with drugs. If Douzi's ad did in fact procure for Belgravia the services of a superstud, and if Douzi did in fact make this super-stud's services available to the female physicists, it's not unreasonable to believe that some of them might have been persuaded to stay. Those who weren't persuaded might either have been killed or forceably detained."

"Very feasible," I confessed.

"So," he went on, "if the Red Chinese theory is valid, as we now believe it is, Douzi is maintaining something of a harem-in-reverse. He has his super-stud servicing the female physicists, and when the dolls aren't being serviced, they're working on the Belgravian nuclear program. It's a master stroke of psychology, and Douzi, as a psychiatrist, is the perfect boy to have dreamed it up."

"But," I reminded him, "you spoke earlier about an extraordinarily sophisticated bomb, a bomb which, if I remember correctly, makes the atom bomb and the hydrogen bomb look in comparison like a couple of Fourth of July firecrackers. Yet, the hydrogen bomb that was exploded on February first is, according to you, less sophisticated than the hydrogen bomb Red China had exploded previously. How do you explain this?"

He smiled sadly. "The bomb exploded on February first was indeed less sophisticated than the Red Chinese hydrogen bomb. But another bomb was exploded in March, and another in May. These last two bombs were, according to the best information available to us, as sophisticated as any bombs either Russia or China has exploded. The new bombs appear to be built on a nitrogen rather than hydrogen base, and their potential for destruction is far greater than that of any bomb any nation, including the United States, has ever exploded. From where we now sit, Belgravia has only to work out certain technicalities and it'll have a bomb far more formidable than anything in the arsenal of any of the world's other five nuclear powers."

"But," I said, "there isn't any real evidence that Belgravia is the developer of the new bomb. So far, all we've got is Red China's theory that this is the case. The theory is plausible, certainly. But mere plausibility doesn't constitute proof."

"You can rest assured, Damon," he replied quietly, "that the United States would be the last country in the world to go along with the theory if Red China hadn't provided some data to back it up. As a matter of fact, they've provided considerable data. While the other four nuclear powers have been observing a strictly hands-off policy toward Belgravia, Red China, thanks to its interest in the Peoples' United Front, has really been in the thick of things. In fact, they've been so much in the thick of things that they've managed to get a spy inside Douzi's harem of female physicists. The spy has provided China with everything from an architect's drawing of the harem to the name of the super-stud on Douzi's payroll."

"And who," I asked, my professional interest aroused, "might that super-stud be?"

"He goes under the name of—believe it or not—Superman. He's a former Cuban, who worked as a male prostitute in Havana during the days of the Batista regime. When Castro took power in 1959, he went into exile and hasn't been heard from since—until he resurfaced in Belgravia this year. According to reports, he's the hottest thing to come along since sex was invented."

"Present company excepted," I amended.

He shook his head. "Present company included, Damon. Far be it from me to demean the talents of America's favorite Coxeman. But I'm afraid that Superman goes even you one better."

"How can he?" I demanded.

"So, it would seem, is Superman. Maybe he's not a priapist. But there's no question that he's a long-distance runner—and he's got one hell of a track record. Back in Havana he used to take on twelve women a night, and send them all away satisfied. That's an impressive score. Furthermore, he's reputedly one of the most generously endowed studs ever created."

"Well," I said cattily, "it's not what you've got but what you do with it that counts."

Walrus-moustache grinned. "Evidently he does quite a bit. Belgravia has developed its bomb, and not one of the nine female physicists has returned to her home country." His eyes twinkled mischievously. "Still, Superman doesn't have your academic background in sexology, so maybe you're a better man than he is. Your country is hoping that you are, because, if you're not, the whole world is in one hell of a fix."

My jaw squared resolutely. "Let me at the nine female physicists. We'll see who's the better man."

"That's precisely what I have in mind. Which brings us to your new mission. As I said, Red China has a spy in the Belgravian harem. She's a twenty-three-year-old cutie named Su Wing, who went to Belgravia to help stir up the Peoples' United Front and somehow or other wound up as President Douzi's mistress. She's a member of CHILLER—our code name for the all-female spy network which is part of Mao's 'Chinese Intelligence and Espionage Agency.' We're going to send you to Africa, where you'll meet CHILLER's *chargé d'affaires* for this caper, a doll named Lin Saong. Once you've proved to her that you're a bona-fide sex expert who can compete with Superman on his own turf, she'll arrange to have Su Wing bring you into the harem. Your job there will be to find out exactly where Douzi is storing his bombs. When you find out, you'll tell Lin Saong, who'll pass the word back to her bosses in Peking. China then will accuse Douzi before the United Nations, and hopefully the UN will be able to intervene before Douzi can get any closer to developing the Big Bomb that could spell curtains for all mankind."

"Wait a minute," I interrupted. "If Su Wing is so close to Douzi, why does Red China need me? And now that I think of it, why would Red China work through the UN—especially since it isn't a member-nation?"

"I'll answer your questions one at a time. First of all, Su Wing is very close to Douzi, but the Belgravian president, a male supremist at heart, won't open up to her about where the bombs are located. Red China can't find out anything more without tipping its hand, and that's why an outside agent—namely you—has to join in on the hunt. We're all hoping that you, by challenging Superman and gaining the confidence of the female physicists, can locate the bombs. Secondly, Red China's motive for working through the UN is simply to become a member of the UN—or so we've been led to believe. We can't overlook the possibility that Mao's people might try something funny once they get the information they want. They probably want the bombs for themselves. But that's the chance we've got to take. Without Red China's missionary work in this caper, we'd be absolutely nowhere. They've approached us on a one-hand-washes-the-other basis. Lacking a better solution to the bomb problem, we've got to take them at their word."

"So," I summarized, "you want me to play footsie with the Red Chinese against a country that may not even be guilty of what we suspect it of, and we all know from the start that we might get double-crossed somewhere along the way."

"Exactly. I'll admit it's not a very desirable arrangement. But it's the arrangement Red China offered us, and when you're the poorboy at the party, you're not in a position to complain about the quality of the hors d'oeuvres."

"But what do we do if Red China does double-cross us?

32

I mean, we're not simply going to accept what they say on blind faith, are we?"

He chuckled softly. "Not quite. According to the deal I worked out with CHILLER, you're supposed to transmit all the information you get to Lin Saong via radio. I'm going to send another Coxeman to Belgravia with you, a man named Dave Wexler. He's the best radioman we have. It'll be his job to learn the beacon you're using to transmit your messages to Lin Saong, then to intercept them. When he does, he'll then cue me in back here in the States. I'll be one step behind you all the way. If Red China tries a double-cross, I'll know about it, and I'll act accordingly. Hopefully the people who are supporting me will be able to undo any damage a double-cross might bring about."

"Hopefully," I echoed. "But judging from the way you describe things, it's a very slim hope."

"It is a very slim hope. But as I said, when you're the poorboy at the party——"

"I know, I know." I heaved a king-sized sigh. "Oh, well, there's one small consolation. At least I won't be getting shot at this time, like in all my other capers for The Coxe Foundation."

His brow furrowed. "Probably not. But before you start feeling too secure, there's something else I've got to tell you. You see, it'd play hell with world public opinion if anyone learned that the United States was cooperating with Red China on this mission. So, while it's extremely unlikely that any dangers will befall you, we in The Coxe Foundation have got to protect ourselves."

"What do you mean?"

"Just this. Under no circumstances are you at any time to reveal to anyone except Lin Saong and the people from CHILLER that you're a U.S. agent. When you show up at the Belgravian harem, CHILLER's inside operative, Su Wing, who has President Douzi believing that she's a double-agent connected with PUF, will tell Douzi that you defected to Red China and that she arranged for you to be sent to Belgravia because she felt that you'd be useful in his enterprise. If all goes well, you'll be permitted to challenge Superman—and you'll get the information Red China and

33

the other nuclear powers want. But if there are any slip-ups, if, for example, Douzi learns that you're a Red Chinese spy, the United States won't be able to bail you out. Once you leave for Belgravia, you're on your own. As far as The Coxe Foundation is concerned, we officially don't know you exist."

"In other words," I gulped, "if Red China pulls a double-cross, I'm the guy in the middle."

"Precisely, Damon," he said sadly. "I'm sorry it has to be this way, but it does. If Douzi ever discovers your secret and if he asks the United States to go to bat for you, we'll back Su Wing's story that you're a defector."

And with these cheery words, he sent me off to Belgravia.

With luck, I'd uncover Douzi's bomb hideout, I'd relay the information to Lin Saong and Red China would take it's claim against Douzi before the United Nations. But if I slipped up I'd either be dead or be branded a traitor. And if I refused to go I'd face a jail sentence.

How did I get into a mess like this?

As I zipped up my pants and prepared to take leave of Lin Saong's hotel room in Port duBeers, I knew the answer. I got into it because a very mature looking sixteen-year-old who lied about her age in one of my research projects opened a door which led to lifetime servitude to The Coxe Foundation.

But there was another, much more important question that remained unanswered. Namely, now that I was in the mess, how the hell was I going to get out of it?

CHAPTER THREE

The car whipped around a sharp curve, then cut off the main highway and down a narrow dirt road. Hunched in a corner of the back seat, my wrists handcuffed behind me, I peered between the pretty heads of the twin cuties up front. The road snaked out before us, wending its way through a mud-thick jungle of lush red and green tropical foliage.

The cutie at the wheel was Girl Number One, who had played Hidden Gully to my Great General Lotus Stalk during the previous night's festivities at Lin Saong's hotel room in Port duBeers. Sharing the front seat with her was Girl Number Two, who had squirmed so deliciously when I solved the riddle of her Mysterious Pearl.

The dynamic duo had picked me up at my hotel room right on schedule at seven a.m. CHILLER-chief Lin Saong had given them a few choice words of instruction. Then I had been dumped into the back seat of their car, and we had set off on the three-hour trek from Port duBeers to President Douzi's harem somewhere on the outskirts of Rodin.

The trip had been an uneventful one. Shortly after we had left Port duBeers, the girls had begun looking at me desiringly, and for a moment I got the impression that they were considering stopping somewhere along the highway for another round of fun and games. But evidently they had decided that they couldn't risk it, because the desiring looks had suddenly stopped. From then on we had traveled in silence.

Now, as we jounced along the bumpy dirt road, Girl Number Two started looking again. At first she confined her glances to my image in the rearview mirror. Then she swiveled around and stared at me directly. Her pert round breasts jiggled sexily against the top of the car seat and her moist pink lips parted invitingly as her pretty almond-shaped eyes did a slow tour of my body.

I smiled at her, and my hips took up a slow, undulating rhythm. Her eyes widened, and her tongue played prettily over the edges of her pearl-white teeth. She hesitated for a moment; then her slender arms reached out toward me, and her hands hovered provocatively over my groin.

I arched my hips to give her a better shot at the target, and she almost scored a bull's-eye. But at the last minute Girl Number One shouted something in Chinese, and my pretty would-be playmate blushingly abandoned the game. I watched, disappointed, as she turned back to face the windshield. She muttered something to Girl Number One, and the plaintive sound of her voice told me that she was as disappointed as I was.

The car negotiated a series of hairpin turns, then slowly climbed a steep, winding hill. The foliage along the road grew thicker, and the limbs of the trees which extended over the roadway were so densely intertwined that only the tiniest flickers of sunlight managed to seep through. We inched a few hundred yards up the hill, and the jungle grew thicker still. Then, slowly, it began thinning out, and we emerged on the hilltop.

I found myself staring down into a valley circled completely by rolling hills. The sight was breathtaking. Like tiers of bleachers in a stadium, circular bands of multi-colored tropical plants spiraled toward the valley's floor. Burbling through the greenery were half a dozen shimmering, finger-thin streams. They met in a small lake, next to which was a vast, carefully manicured garden. In the center of the garden was a complex of four-story buildings, positioned around a septangular courtyard. A few hundred yards away from the complex was another cluster of buildings, these considerably smaller. And a few hundred yards from them was a third cluster, smaller still.

A strange sense of *déjà vu* overcame me. The scene was more than vaguely familiar, and I wondered where and when I'd viewed it before.

36

Then suddenly I remembered. It had been in Turkey eight years ago. I was studying Topkapi Sarayi, the famous pleasure palace of Muhammad II, fifteenth century ruler of the Ottoman empire.

Muhammad didn't invent the word "harem," but he might as well have, because the word, as it's used today, describes exactly the sort of multi-girl living arrangement which Muhammad raised to a fine art.

In 1454, shortly after Muhammad's troops had taken Constantinople, the Ottoman chief built a palace on that city's well-known Third Hill. Being an energetic debauchee but also a man who liked to keep his distance from his womenfolk when he wasn't folking with them, he divided the palace into two sections. The first, consisting of his library, his dining room, his bedroom and other rooms which he wished to enjoy in privacy, was called *selamlik*, a Turkish word which translates approximately as "domain of the husband." The second section, where his women were quartered, was called *haremlik*, which translates as "domain of the wife."

In Muhammad's case, of course, there was more than one wife. Indeed, according to the Italian writer, Domenico Hierosolimitano, in *Relatione della gran città di Costantinopoli* (circa 1595) there were all of three hundred and seventy wives—and a hundred and twenty-seven eunuchs to keep them in line. Each evening, Muhammad would venture into the haremlik, bed down with one or more of the three hundred and seventy dolls, then retire to his selamlik for meditation, contemplation and, presumably, rest. Occasionally he would also offer the girls' services to one or more of his friends. But at no time were the girls permitted to take lovers other than those assigned to them by Muhammad. In fact, from the moment they entered the haremlik, they were not permitted to leave until Muhammad tired of their charms and sent them on their way once and for all.

After Muhammad's death, succeeding generations of Turkish rulers occupied the palace on the Third Hill and reveled amidst the pretties of the haremlik. Eventually the palace was abandoned, but the haremlik tradition contin-

37

ued until 1909, when Abdul-Hamid II, the last of the Ottoman emperors, was deposed. By this time the word, haremlik, had been shortened to harem, and had come to mean not a section of a house reserved for women but rather the institution of keeping a number of wives.

Now, in Belgravia, the institution was being continued by Dr. Albert Douzi, except that in his harem the "wives" were being served rather than doing the serving. However, while gender status might have been reversed, Douzi apparently was extremely faithful to the physical trappings whereunder the harem originated. As the car in which I was riding started down the winding road toward the floor of the valley, I could see that the President of Belgravia had duplicated exactly the buildings and the gardens of old Muhammad II's fifteenth century palace, Topkapi Sarayi, in Constantinople.

I wondered why he'd gone to the trouble. According to everything I'd been told by Walrus-moustache and Lin Saong, Douzi's only interest in the harem idea was as a means of keeping the nine female physicists working on his bomb. Superman's place in this scheme of things was logical enough. And it was conceivable that Douzi might have taken a few other pains to keep his physicist femmes happy—like showering them with diamonds from the duBeers mines. But what kicks would the girls get out of living in a carefully reconstructed palace the historical significance of which they probably didn't even know about? And if the palace hadn't been built for the benefit of the physicists, for whose benefit had it been built?

I was still wondering when my car pulled to a halt in front of a huge iron gate. A tall, slim, rifle-toting, black-skinned guard in a khaki uniform and pith helmet stepped from behind the gate and approached Girl Number One at the steering wheel. She handed him a slip of paper, which he read. Then he retreated to a small guardhouse and made a phone call.

A few minutes later another car appeared at the opposite side of the gate. A tiny Oriental girl with delicate features stepped out of the back seat. She said something to the guard, who bowed politely in reply. Then she came over to my car.

As she walked, a gentle breeze blew her multicolored silky kimono against her. My breath caught in my throat as my eyes took in every curve of her succulent body. Her firm, round breasts nestled snugly under the soft, smooth fabric of the garment, and her slender legs stretched out enticingly before her, each step more compellingly drawing my attention to the Golden Crevice which lay at their apex, and which now was outlined so clearly against the windblown kimono that I could discern every delicious nook and cranny of its tantalizing topography.

She said something in Chinese to my traveling companions. Then Girl Number One ushered me out of the back seat and unlocked my handcuffs, while Girl Number Two opened the car trunk and took out my suitcase. The wind had stopped blowing by this time, so I raised my eyes from the kimono and I gave a smile of greeting. "Su Wing?" I asked, knowing the answer well in advance.

She smiled back. "It's a pleasure to meet you, Dr. Damon. I'm sorry we didn't make each other's acquaintance under less strained circumstances. But then, one cannot always have things as one would like them, can one?"

"No," I admitted, "one cannot."

She gestured toward the gate. I shot Girl Number One and Girl Number Two a lascivious parting glance. Then I followed Su Wing to her car. She said something to the driver in a language I assumed to be one of the Belgravian tribal tongues, and we sped off.

"We haven't much time to talk," she told me once we were on our way, "so I'll speak quickly. I assume that Lin Saong has briefed you thoroughly about all the details of the mission and how to transmit your findings to her."

"She has."

"Fine. I'll add a few comments about the general situation at the palace. Then, if you have any questions, we can discuss them. However, once you've become situated at the palace, we must keep our contact to a minimum. There you will speak to me only when absolutely necessary

39

and only when we're somewhere where we're not likely to be overheard."

"Don't worry," I said. "I don't want to get discovered any more than you do."

Her smile told me that she was glad she was doing business with a fellow non-hero. It also told me, unless my imagination was playing tricks on me, that she wouldn't mind testing my much-touted sexual expertise if the opportunity arose. I let my leg slide casually across the seat until it came to rest against the soft firmness of her kimono-draped thigh. She returned my pressure, and her smile broadened. I decided that my imagination wasn't playing any tricks whatsoever.

The car turned down a narrow, tree-shaded lane. We passed a cluster of marble statues beneath a pomegranate tree. "Pretend you're admiring the scenery," Su Wing said. "I've told the driver to take us on a tour of the grounds. That should give us five or ten minutes to talk. He doesn't understand English, so he'll have no idea of what we're saying."

Playing the gimmick for all it was worth, I enthusiastically said, "Those are marvelous statues. Really nice. So realistic too. Just beautiful." My hand found her thigh, and I began stroking it gently. "I don't think I've ever seen anything so beautiful—I mean—well, you know what I mean."

"Damon," she said softly, "you do appreciate the finer things." But she made no move to stop my caresses.

I found the hem of her kimono. My fingers inched their way underneath and began stroking the smooth, golden flesh of her calf. "Lovely legs," I babbled on. "A marvel of Oriental sculpture. Exquisite lines, scrumptuous texture, fantastic form . . . "

She wriggled delightedly under my touch. "Damon, if you keep on doing this, you're going to get me all excited and I won't be able to give you my briefing."

My palm massaged the gentle slope where her neatly rounded calf merged with the creamy soft underside of her knee. Then I slowly advanced up the shapely pillar of her thigh. "Excited?" I teased. "I thought you CHILLER la-

40

dies didn't get excited about anything but Chairman Mao's platitudes. Do you mean to tell me that a warm, sexy woman lurks beneath the icy facade of Party Member Su Wing? Or are you an impostor, someone who killed the real Su Wing and took her place in the harem to thwart PUF's plans to overthrow Dr. Douzi's government?"

Her hips slid forward on the seat, urging my hand toward the warm, moist well of her womanhood. "I'm the real Su Wing. And whether I'm supposed to or not, I love sex. But, Damon"—her body tensed, and her face took on a worried look—"we shouldn't be playing around like this in the car. The driver might see us."

"He can't. The parts of our bodies that're doing the playing are out of his line of vision." I grinned, and my hand shot up her thigh until it could go no farther. She wasn't wearing panties. The sweet dampness of her Sacred Field inundated me.

"Okay, we'll play," she gasped, squirming fiercely under my touch. "But for heaven's sake let's talk business while we do. There isn't much time left, and I must brief you completely before I introduce you to Dr. Douzi."

My fingers parted the Sacred Field's succulent furrows, then slowly slipped inside. "Begin the briefing," I said, wriggling two fingers provocatively.

A spasm of pleasure shook her entire body. "I will," she moaned. "I mean, I want to. But I—uh, Damon . . . ahhhhhh . . . oh, Damon . . ."

"The briefing," I reminded her, working my way even farther inside her. "Begin the briefing."

"Uhhhhhhhh," she replied. "Oooooohhhhh. Ahhhhhhhhhh ! ! !"

The car rounded another turn. We passed an ornate Byzantine fountain, surrounded by flaming-purple tropical plants. I was sure that the driver couldn't take too many more of those "ooohhh's" and "ahhhhhh's" without becoming suspicious, so I began ad-libbing. "Lovely fountain there. Really beautiful." My fingers probed deeper inside Su Wing's Golden Crevice, and my palm rubbed gently against the soft down of her Mount of Venus. "Lovely foliage, too. Just marvelous."

41

Su Wing slid across the seat until both of us were wedged into one corner. Pointing at the fountain with a trembling index finger, she stammered: "I-it's a f-fifteenth century treasure, imported from T-turkey. Dr. Douzi received it as a, a—ahhhhh, Damon, that feels so good!—as a g-gift from the T-turkish government."

With my free hand, I unzipped my fly. Then I eased her leg over my hips. There was a moment of frantic fumbling as my Jade Stalk searched for her Sacred Scabard. Then she pressed hard against my urgently upthrust hips, and I was immersed to the hilt.

"Ohhhhhhhh!" she sighed. "Ohhhhhhhhhh! Oooooooo-ooooo!" Then, presumably for the driver's benefit, she added quickly, "Dr. Douzi has always been a connoisseur of Turkish culture. He's studied the Ottoman empire extensively."

My hips took up a quick front-and-back movement. With each thrust, her super-sexy body quivered more violently. "I'm something of a connoisseur myself," I quipped. "And so, it would seem, are you."

"But, Damon," she panted, suddenly remembering what we were supposed to be doing, "the tour of the grounds is half over, and I haven't even begun to brief you."

"Then begin," I grunted, thrusting harder. "And tell the driver to slow down. We need all the time we can get."

Digging her fingernails into my thigh, she barked something at the driver. His mumbled reply suggested that he was completely in the dark as to what was going on behind his back.

I glanced at his rearview mirror. His eyes were glued to the road. Through the mirror I could see only down as far as the lapels on his khaki uniform. That meant that he could see not much farther down the bodies of Su Wing and me. If he chanced to look at us, all he'd know was that the two of us were sitting side-by-side, Su Wing pointing out the windows at the *objets d'art* along the roadway and I watching with what appeared to be rapt attention. But the picture south of the border was a horse of a different color. Color it groovy.

Su Wing's hips were flopping back and forth in a mad

42

mambo of carnal abandonment. One of her legs was coiled tightly around my thigh. The other was hooked around my opposite calf. With each movement of her hips, both legs squeezed me hard, then relaxed their grip. The action sent shock waves of sensation coursing through my body.

"N-now then, Damon," she was saying, "on with the briefing. I came to Belgravia in—in—oh, Damon, that thing you're doing now is exquisite—I—ahhhhhh—I came to Belgravia—oh, yes, keep doing it like that—I—I—ahhhhh—"

I could see that we weren't going to make much headway with the briefing until she got her rocks off. But I frankly didn't care. It wasn't that I was indifferent to the state of affairs in the Belgravian harem. It was just that I had a few affairs of my own to settle first.

Pressing my feet against the floorboards for support, I began hammering at her more violently. The scalding hot sheath of her Hidden Gully jerked my Ivory Scepter this way and that. Inside me, a fiery ball of passion strained for release. I hammered harder, and the Moment of Truth drew closer.

"Damon!" she gasped suddenly. "Oh, Damon!" The frantic flopping of her hips and the wild scissorlike movements of her legs told me that The Moment was even closer for her than it was for me. I wondered idly what kind of a loser Dr. Albert Douzi must be in bed if his mistress could get this hot this soon with me. But I didn't wonder for long, because the same spasms of orgasmic ecstasy that heralded her trip over the top had all of a sudden taken possession of me.

My fingers clutched at her fast-moving hips, pulling them hard against me. My Jade Stem reached deeper and deeper inside her. For an instant I hovered precariously at the brink of pleasure. Then, in an explosion of bliss, I plunged off the deep end.

The sensation was scrumptuous. Every cell of my body tingled with delight. Her whole body tugged at me hungrily, as if trying to squeeze out every last drop of love's sweet juices. I savored the feeling as long as it lasted. Then, slowly, I coasted down from my sex-high, and my hips resumed their previous low-gear gyrations.

She fell into rhythm with me. Then, after a few seconds, her body tensed and all movement stopped. A worried look distorted her pretty face. "We're at the palace, Damon," she whispered urgently. "The tour is over."

The car was approaching a gravel drive leading to the port cochere in front of an ornate Byzantine mansion. I glanced at the building, then at the mirror-image of our chauffeur's unseeing eyes. "Tell the driver I'd like another trip around the circuit," I said, thinking quickly. "Then let's get on with the briefing."

Obediently she conveyed the instructions to the super-stoic man behind the wheel. Unblinkingly he steered past the drive and back onto the main roadway. Su Wing relaxed, and her hips swung back into action. I relaxed with her, and my hip-tempo quickened to match hers.

"Now then," she said, pointing absently toward the bust of a black warrior on a pedestal surrounded by exotic shrubbery, "this is the general situation. I was sent by China to Belgravia in 1966. Because I'm young and sexually attractive, and because I speak English and French as well as Chinese and several Belgravian tribal tongues, I was selected as the person who would attempt to infiltrate Dr. Douzi's government on behalf of the Peoples' United Front. According to the plan, Douzi's people would be led to believe that I was the leader of the female detachment which had been sent by China to aid PUF. Actually, of course, Lin Saong was—and is—the commander, and I was—and am—only an underling. But my superiors believed that I could function most effectively if the Belgravians thought I was in charge of the entire operation. Their reasoning was that once Douzi's people had captured me they would attempt to use me as a spy against my own cause. Then, by pretending to go along with the arrangement, I could spy on Douzi."

"In other words," I put in, "you were supposed to function as a triple agent."

"Exactly, and that's just what happened. A short while after the rumor was spread that I had come to Belgravia to take over China's female detachment of PUF advisors, I let

44

myself get captured by BELSO, the Belgravian Security Organization, Douzi's secret police. I was tortured for information about PUF, and I supplied it. Not information that would hurt PUF's cause, naturally, but nonetheless enough information for BELSO to think it had scored a real victory. Presently I was brought before BELSO's commander, General Pierre Mariba. He told me that I'd be killed unless I agreed to go along with a plan he had worked out. According to the plan, I'd return to PUF in my old capacity as leader of the Chinese female detachment. Then I'd continue to feed BELSO information about PUF's operations. At the same time, BELSO would give me information about the Douzi government—information which would be useful to PUF. Thus PUF would think I was spying on Douzi's government while actually I would be spying *for* Douzi's government and against PUF. This was precisely the arrangement I had hoped to establish, so after offering token resistance I told General Mariba that I'd do his bidding. That's how my career as a triple agent began."

"How did you manage to get Douzi to accept you as his mistress?"

"That's a long story. Actually the whole thing was a stroke of luck. Among the tortures which BELSO employed to get me to reveal the information it desired were a number of sexual tortures. I was assaulted sexually and was forced to entertain my captors with a number of sex acts which would make the average girl shudder with revulsion. The acts didn't make me shudder, however, because I was long accustomed to performing them. You see, back in China, before I became a member of the spy organization which you Americans refer to as CHILLER, I had been a prostitute. In fact, it was under threat of being executed as a prostitute that I consented to join the CHILLER organization."

"Su Wing," I observed, "you and I have a lot more in common than a love for sex."

"Yes, I know. Your government told my government how you had been coerced into becoming a spy, and word of what happened was passed down through Lin Saong to
45

me." She flashed a comradely smile. "Anyway, I lent myself enthusiastically to the sex acts that the BELSO people wanted me to perform, and gradually rumors of my sexual expertise spread upward through channels. After the BELSO interrogators in Port duBeers ravished me, I was handed over to the Port duBeers commander. He then handed me over to General Mariba, who eventually handed me over to Professor Robert Akaba, President Douzi's Minister of Internal Affairs. After Akaba, I made the rounds of other Cabinet members, and finally I was handed over to President Douzi himself. He liked me so much that he asked me to become his mistress. He pointed out that I could assume the role without any difficulty, since PUF would think I was doing so only in the interest of spying on Belgravia. Actually, that was precisely my motivation, so I moved in as Douzi's mistress, and I've been his mistress ever since."

"But, as his mistress, aren't you in a better position than I ever would be to discover where the super-bomb is being stored?"

She sighed. "I'm afraid not. While Dr. Douzi may not suspect that I'm a double-agent, he nonetheless is very cautious. He knows that I must communicate constantly with the CHILLER agents whom he assumes to be my subordinates, but he monitors my transmissions. Also, I am never permitted to leave the palace unless I'm accompanied by one of the eunuchs on Douzis staff—a fellow who speaks all the languages I speak and who would know instantly if I attempted to double-cross Douzi. The fact that the fellow's a eunuch, and a homosexual to boot, makes it impossible for me to employ my feminine wiles on him. Finally, Douzi doesn't permit me to associate with the female nuclear physicists, who are the only people in the palace—with the possible exception of Superman—who know where the bomb laboratory is located. The physicists, of course, never leave the palace grounds, so I assume that the laboratory is located in one of the buildings inside these gates. But which building? I can only guess. Also, it's quite unlikely that the developed bombs are stored in the bomb laboratory or in other buildings on

46

the palace grounds. Most probably they're stored somewhere in the Belgravian interior. It's the location of these bombs that's so important to CHILLER, and that's why China agreed to cooperate with the United States in getting you into the physicists' harem. You've got to find these bombs."

"But," I protested, "how am I supposed to find them? Even if I do prove that I'm a better man than Superman—and I think I will prove it—why would the physicists tell me where the bombs are? As a matter of fact, the physicists themselves may not know where they are."

She nodded sadly. "That's the chance we have to take, Damon. And I'm taking as big a chance as you are. We both know that PUF will assault Belgravia if the bombs aren't found. The assault will explode the bombs, killing everyone in the country—including you and me."

I groaned. "And to think I gave up the prospects of a comfortable jail cell in the United States for this."

Her groan echoed mine. "Don't feel bad. I gave up a comfortable bed in a Peking whorehouse. But we're in this together now, and its up to us to get ourselves out of it. I'll do my part. I only hope you can do yours." Smiling mirthlessly, she tightened her vaginal muscles, giving my Jade Staff a reassuring squeeze. "You've got the equipment, Damon, and heaven knows, you know how to use it. Let's just hope Douzi's physicists like you as much as I do."

"They will," I said confidently. "The question is, will they like me enough to tell me where the bomb is—if they know."

Our car again passed the Byzantine fountain surrounded by flaming-purple tropical plants. We were at the halfway point in our second turn around the garden, and I was pretty sure we couldn't hope for a third. Stoic though he might be, our driver simply couldn't be gullible enough to accept that sort of request without becoming suspicious.

"Okay," I told Su Wing, "so much for the dangers that await us. Now how do I go about getting into the harem and challenging Superman on his own turf."

She smiled. "All that has been worked out. When I learned that the United States would cooperate with China by sending you on this mission, I told Douzi that you had defected to the Chinese because the United States wouldn't give you enough freedom to conduct your sexual experiments."

I gulped. "He accepted an improbable story like that?"

"He was suspicious, to be sure. He knows, as do both you and I, that China is hardly the most sexually liberal country in the world. However, I fabricated a few details about your being an enthusiastic admirer of Chairman Mao and a bitter enemy of American imperialism. I also reminded him that you'd be very useful to him in his harem. The last point, I think, is what sold him. When I said I could arrange to have my superiors assign you to Belgravia to work for me, he practically leapt at the opportunity to get you here."

"But, if Superman is as good as I'm told he is, what does Douzi want with me? Or is Superman not quite so super as people say?"

"He's very super. I haven't made love to him myself, but according to what I hear, he's a real champion. The problem is that he's too much of a champion."

"I don't follow you."

"Well, to put it bluntly, the female physicists just can't get enough of him. He takes on all nine of them every night. Each girl gets one hour with him. In the early days of the bomb project, this was enough to satisfy them. But now they want more. They compete with each other constantly to see who'll be the first one of the night to have him, and they're always trying to bribe him into spending some of his off-duty hours with them. The competition has become so fierce that it's affecting their work. Douzi hasn't really discussed the matter with me, but I can tell from what I've heard here and there that progress on the bombs has slowed down considerably in the recent weeks. I suspect that Douzi thinks you'll help calm the girls down. If they've got both you and Superman servicing them, they'll spend more time in the laboratory. That'll put the bomb project back on schedule, and everybody in Douzi's regime can breathe easier once again."

"But does Douzi actually believe I'll go along with his

plans? I mean, if I'm an idealistic defector to Communism, shouldn't I be reluctant to help out a man who's very much opposed to the Communist ideal?"

"As far as Douzi is concerned, you don't know what his plans are. All you know is that there are nine girls who need your sexual services. You're aware, of course, that Belgravia is not a Communist country. But you believe that it soon will be, thanks to PUF. So you're entering the harem thinking that it'll be a nice place to spend your time until the day of the peoples' revolution finally dawns."

I scratched my head. "This is getting very confusing."

"True. But the espionage game always is. Suffice it to say at this point that Douzi doesn't supsect you. If you can manage to act as though your only interest is sex, you won't give him reason to change his opinion. And if you can excite the nine physicists as much as Superman excites them, you may just be able to find out where the bombs are being stored." Her eyes took on a fervent look. "Your life depends on it, Damon. And so does mine. And so does the security of the world."

Our car rounded a turn and headed up a slight incline. In the distance I could see the spires of the mansion which represented the terminal point of our second turn around the grounds. Su Wing's briefing was over, but there still was some unfinished business at hand, namely the business of love-making. While she had been briefing me, both of us had continued sexing. Now the hot sparks of passion were beginning once again to glow inside me, and I had only a few minutes to fan them into flame.

Clutching her luxuriously soft thighs, I began to thrust more vigorously. She promptly matched my strokes, and passion's sparks began to glow more brightly. The mansion drew nearer, and I thrust harder. Then, a few hundred yards from the port cochere, I felt the familiar warm sensation that told me orgasm was fast approaching. I picked up the pace of my movements until my groin was athrob with electric tongues of sensation. Then, in a mad burst of speed, I raced across the finish line.

Su Wing realized what was happening. "Damon!" she gasped. "Wait for me!"

But she was too late. The words were barely out of her mouth when the car rounded the gravel drive in front of the mansion.

"Damn!" she said disgustedly.

"Better luck next time," I grinned, helping her off her passionately quivering perch. She was pouting.

She tugged her kimono back down over her legs just as the car came to a halt. I zipped my fly. My work on this harem affair was about to begin in earnest.

CHAPTER FOUR

"Welcome, Dr. Damon, to Belgravia, and may your stay be a long and pleasant one. Every effort will be made while you are here to insure your comfort. All that I ask in return is that you satisfy the female guests of my household. Presently I shall introduce you to these guests and give you the opportunity to demonstrate your sexual prowess. Meanwhile, permit me to inquire as to how you happen to come among us."

The speaker was Dr. Albert Douzi, President of Belgravia.

The place of our meeting was his study, a massive and ornately decorated room on the fourth floor of the palace.

Before being introduced to him I hadn't formed an impression of what he might be like physically. But I had assumed that he'd be more or less normal.

I'd been wrong. Douzi was a pygmy. He stood no taller than four feet and couldn't have weighed more than eighty-five or ninety pounds. Sitting behind his massive mahogany desk, decked out in a braided white uniform resplendent with medals and military decorations, he looked less like a head of state than like a child dressed up in an expensive soldier-suit. Even his face was childlike—smooth, round and cherubic. Only his long, straight, steel gray hair and his deep bass voice testified to the fact that he was an adult.

After I overcame the initial shock of his appearance, my interview with him went precisely as Su Wing had led me to believe it would.

I gave him the cover story about my defecting to Red China because the United States wouldn't allow me the freedom I wanted to conduct my sexual experiments. He accepted it without question.

I told him that my contacts in China had sent me to Belgravia because Su Wing had told them that his harem of female physicists would be an ideal place for me to conduct further sexual investigations. He accepted this without question also.

I filled him in on my work with the League for Sexual Dynamics, and I spelled out the details of some of my earlier studies. He listened intently, and he questioned me at length about the reactions of my female subjects to my love-making. But he never said anything that indicated he was suspicious of me.

Finally the interview was over. Smiling hospitably, Douzi led the way down a flight of stairs. We passed through a white marble corridor into an opulently appointed three-room apartment.

Again a feeling of *déjà vu* overcame me, just as it had when I first looked down the hill at the royal palace and its grounds. But this time I didn't have to think twice about where I'd seen what I was seeing. The apartment was an exact replica of *Hünkâr Hamami*, the sultan's bath in the sixteenth century palace of Muhammad II.

The first room was a large foyer with white marble walls, the linear purity of which was broken only by an octet of tall, narrow columns topped with ornate capitals. Between the columns were low sofas, upholstered in elegant gold and silver embroidered patterns and laden with soft, goose-feather cushions. Heavy persian rugs covered the floors. In the *Hünkâr Hamami* of Muhammad II, this room served as a dressing room and its walls were festooned with gold tapestries encrusted with strings of white pearls. Douzi evidently had been unable to procure copies of the tapestries; but he had duplicated Muhammad's foyer in every other detail, including a jewel-studded *nargileh*, or Turkish water pipe, and a coffee set which stood on a clean-lined low ebony table near the door opposite the entrance.

Form the foyer, my pint-sized host led me to a second room, the *tepidarium*, or warm water bath. Here again the walls were of white marble, and the doorway was flanked with slender white columns. The wall on the left supported an ornate marble fountain, the gold faucets of which were lions' heads spitting water into a twelve-foot-square marble tub in the center of the floor. The wall on the right was given over to a Byzantine mosaic depicting an enormous black man being teased sexually by a trio of pink-skinned girls. The first girl was rubbing her breasts against the side of his face, while the second was licking his belly and the third was licking his thighs. His upthrust penis testified to the efficacy of the girls' techniques.

The third and final room was the *calidarium,* or hot water bath. It was twice as large as the first two rooms combined, and its decor was easily three times as opulent. On the wall opposite the door was a huge fountain with five gold lions' heads which spit boiling hot water into a marble tub that measured all of twenty feet square. The tub was raised on a marble step. At each end was a high-backed marble bench with a single armrest. In each corner of the room was a small wall fountain decorated with gold, and surrounding each fountain was a cluster of marble stools. From the stools a person could watch the proceedings in the tub or could look out a window at the neatly manicured shrubbery of the garden below.

My appreciative eyes took in the details of the room. Then I turned to Douzi and smiled. "My compliments," I said. "Muhammad II would feel quite at home here."

His tiny, childlike face took on an expression of amazement. "You recognize the source of my inspiration?" he beamed. "Then you really are a sex expert. I'd venture to say there aren't two dozen men alive who would realize so quickly that my palace is a replica of *Topkapi Sarayi.*" He led the way to one of the marble benches alongside the tub and gestured for me to sit beside him. "Ever since I saw the palace at Constantinople," he went on, "I've dreamed of recreating it. It took me nearly six years, but false modesty aside, I'll venture to say that I've done a very good job."

"Very good indeed," I agreed. "I can't wait to see what you've done in some of the other rooms."

"You shall, Dr. Damon, and in very short order." He

53

smiled proudly. "Half the joy of accomplishment is in sharing one's works with persons who appreciate them. Though you and I have known each other only a few minutes, I can say confidently that I have found in you a truly kindred spirit." He reached for a pull-cord alongside the bench and gave it a sharp tug. A bell rang in a nearby room. "And now I have a real treat in store for you. As Su Wing undoubtedly mentioned, I've arranged a welcome celebration. Right now, in this very bath, I shall stage for your pleasure one of the most exciting sexual rituals ever known to man, a ritual known as the 'fountain of youth.' Have you ever heard ot it?"

I nodded. "It was one of Muhammad II's favorites—or so we're led to believe by students of the Ottoman empire. Actually there's no concrete evidence that the rite was performed in the sixteenth century. But it was introduced in Paris brothels during the nineteenth century by girls who had been bought from the harem of Abd ul-Hamid II, the last of the Ottoman emperors, and it resembles very closely a number of other rites which were unquestionably the invention of Muhammad II himself."

Douzi's little-boy's face glowed with a mixture of astonishment and camaraderie.

"Damon," he said, "I cannot tell you how gratifying it is to meet a fellow connoisseur. So many men today claim to be devotees of libertinage, but so few have any real knowledge of the sexual arts. I hope for the sake of my female house guests that your performance is on par with your academic background."

"It is," I assured him. "That's my stock in trade." Then, seizing the opportunity to get him talking about the female physicists, I added, "Tell me something about these house guests. Who are they? And why do you want me to entertain them sexually?"

His smile was cordial, but it didn't mask the fact that I'd ventured into an area he really didn't care to talk about.

"The girls," he said after a moment, "are just friends of mine. Perhaps it would be more accurate to say that they are friends of my nation and that it is my responsibility to keep them happy while they are here. In any case, you need not trouble yourself about their identity or their reasons for being here. I will be quite content if you concentrate on satisfying them physically."

"But," I pressed, not willing to let him off the hook so easily, "physical satisfaction is inextricably intertwined with emotional and intellectual compatibility. Unless I know something about them, I won't be able to do my best."

His expression hardened. "For the time being, Damon, I can tell you nothing more. Establish whatever emotional and intellectual rapport with the girls that you can, but don't inquire too closely into their personal histories. The less you know about their background, the better off you'll be."

I would've probed further. But just then a pair of Buddha-fat Nubian giants wearing floor-length white silk robes waddled into the room and knelt at Douzi's feet. "My eunuch," he explained, placing a hand gently on each one's head. "They've come to undress us for the afternoon's ritual."

Resolving to pursue the matter of the female physicists later, I surrendered my attentions completely to the matter at hand.

No sooner had the enormous eunuchs knelt at their diminutive master's feet than a pair of tiny black men entered the room. Neither was taller than four feet, and both were decked out in flaming red silk pantaloons and bright orange turbans. At first glance they appeared to be children, but a closer look revealed age-lines around their eyes and mouths. They were, like Douzi, pygmies. Each carried a jewel-studded *nargileh*.

The two men were followed immediately by a pygmy girl. She also wore flaming red silk pantaloons, but nothing else. Her long black hair toppled provocatively over her shoulders and around the gently curved slopes of her full, exquisitely formed breasts. Her nipples were jet black and stood erect. She carried a miniature *sitar*, or Turkish guitar.

Douzi clapped his hands twice and the girl sat cross-legged at the edge of the tub. Cradling the *sitar* in her lap, she gently stroked its strings. Then, contrapuntally to the instrument's fast-moving melody line, she began humming an eerie chant.

As if on cue, the two pygmy men materialized alongside Douzi and me. Douzi was given the stem of one pipe and I was given the stem of the other. The pipes were lit, and the sweet, pungent aroma of hashish filled the room.

Douzi puffed energetically, sucking the smoke deeply into his lungs, then holding it inside him for all of thirty seconds before letting go. I followed his lead. Almost immediately an airy light-headedness took hold of me. My muscles relaxed and I found myself staring at the breasts of the pygmy girl with intense admiration. Never, it seemed, had I seen such beautiful breasts, such well-sculptured breasts, such delectable breasts. I didn't especially want to touch them; I was content merely to look at them and bask in their beauty.

My host and I smoked for perhaps five minutes. With each minute I grew more relaxed and more appreciative of my surroundings. I remembered experiencing a feeling something like this back when I smoked marijuana as part of my work on *The Big Freak-Out,* but the feeling wasn't one one-hundredth as intense as it was now. No doubt about it, I told myself, Douzi uses high-quality hash. The thought wasn't especially funny, but I found myself laughing uproariously at it. Douzi, though he couldn't possibly know what I was laughing at, amiably laughed along with me.

Finally the pint-sized President handed the stem of his pipe to the pygmy who stood at his side. I likewise surrendered my stem, and the two pygmies retreated to a corner of the room. Douzi then clapped his hands twice more, and the two eunuchs, who had knelt motionless at his feet during the entire smoking session, slowly stood up.

I watched with interest as the obese giants peeled off their white silk robes. Each man stood over six feet and each weighed all of three hundred pounds. Their bellies hung over their white loincloths, and great blobs of loose flesh dangled where their arm and leg muscles ordinarily would be. Folding the robes and placing them carefully on a stool, the immense creatures bowed toward Douzi. Then, like a well-choreographed dance team, they stood erect and reached for the knots which fastened their loincloths. Douzi nudged me with his elbow. "This," he smiled, "has always been one of my favorite parts of the ritual."

I wondered idly why a man who presumably was heterosexual would get a kick out of watching a pair of eunuchs drop their drawers. But I didn't dwell on the matter. I was so wrapped up in my hashish high that my predominant feeling was one of sympathetic pleasure. It made me happy that the drawer-dropping routine would make Douzi happy.

Also, I was kind of curious as to what I'd see when the loincloths finally came down. In the course of my sexual studies, I had learned that there were three varieties of eunuchs. The first type, called *thlibias* or *semivirs* in the classic Sanskirt, had had their testicles amputated, bruised, crushed or otherwise permanently damaged. Thus they were rendered sterile, but they still were able to achieve penile erection and to copulate. The second group, called *spadones,* retained their testicles but had lost their penises. Thus, while technically fertile, they lacked the ability to achieve normal sexual pleasure, although some learned to satisfy themselves homosexually as the recipient partner in oral or anal sex acts. The third group, called *sandali,* were in worse shape yet. The term, *sandali,* translates as "clean-shaven," and that's exactly what these unfortunate creatures were. After one's penis and testicles had been sliced off with a razor, a tube was placed in his urethra and the wound was cauterized with boiling oil; in some cases, flesh would then grow around the protruding tip of the tube, and the eunuch's groin would very much resemble the female genitalia. Like *spadones,* the *sandali* had no way to achieve normal sexual pleasure, although some learned to satisfy themselves via oral or anal homosexual acts. I wondered which type of eunuch Douzi's two giants would be.

They were, I soon found out, *sandali.* As their loin-clothes dropped away from their hips, I could see that their pubic hair gave way to a pair of tender-looking fleshy growths very similar to a female's *labia majora.* Both eunuchs seemed to shudder as these growths were exposed to our eyes, and Douzi giggled gleefully at their reaction.

"They've been eunuchs for years now," he chortled, nudging me in the ribs, "but they're still embarrassed to expose themselves. Isn't that hilarious?"

I laughed, but this time it was strictly an act. The hashish high notwithstanding, my sympathies lay with the eunuchs rather than with their sadistic mini-master.

Now completely naked, the black giants knelt again. One began untying my shoelaces, while the other went to work on the buckles of Douzi's knee-high black leather boots. Cackling evilly, Douzi kept pulling the boot away from the profusely sweating eunuch's fumbling fingers. Finally the black giant lost his balance and stumbled forward on all fours, whereupon Douzi's tiny leg stiffened and his boot cracked jarringly into his hapless victim's jaw.

The eunuch bolted upright. His hands shot up to his face, and a soft whimper escaped from his throat. Douzi, cackling louder than ever, barked something in a Belgravian tribal language. The giant, tears rolling down his cheeks, bent once again to his task.

"Don't be afraid to treat the devils roughly," Douzi told me. "They respond best to harshness."

But I was too repelled by the cruelty to continue playing the role of the amiable guest. "Muhammed II abhorred harshness," I said, not concealing my disgust. "He believed that eunuchs and women should be treated with the utmost gentleness."

Douzi's jaw muscles tightened. "You're not in Muhammad's palace, Damon. You're in mine." His eyes were looking daggers at me.

"I'll take my pleasures my own way," I said evenly. "If you don't like it, you can always send me back to China."

His eyes narrowed. Evidently he hadn't anticipated that I'd be anything but totally acquiescent. For a moment neither of us said anything. Then, slowly, his small mouth spread in a tight, tense smile. "Very well," he said softly, "do things your way. But remember, you're not an ordinary guest here. In the future I may decide to make cer-

58

tain demands of you, demands that won't necessarily be to your liking. You'll have no choice but to carry out my orders. I trust you're prepared to do so."

I let a moment pass. Then I said, "We'll talk about that when the time comes."

He hesitated, as if wondering whether to make a further attempt to assert his superiority. Then he evidently decided not to. Turning to his eunuch he mumbled something in Belgravian. The eunuch quickly slipped off both boots, and the undressing ritual continued.

After my shoes were off, my eunuch went to work on my trousers. As he slid them over my hips, he brought his face to my groin and pressed hard. The feel of his flabby flesh against my manhood was anything but pleasant. But I was interested in getting the ritual over as quickly as possible, so I said nothing. The eunuch, keeping his face buried between my thighs, promptly removed my socks, then slid off my shorts.

My sex now exposed, the black giant straddled my legs with his thighs and began removing my jacket. As he did, he rubbed against me with the fleshy folds that were where his amputated genitalia once had been. My repulsion intensified, but I still made no attempt to stop him. Instead, I quickly slipped my arms out of the jacket sleeves and began unbuttoning my shirt while the eunuch undid my tie.

After what seemed like an eternity, my shirt was off and so was my T-shirt. The eunuch then crouched in front of me and wetly kissed my belly and thighs while his fingers stroked my buttocks. By this time I was so sick of the whole business that I wanted to vomit. But I forced myself to keep my emotions in check. I wasn't sure just how resistant I could be without getting Douzi mad enough to send me on my way—and a one-way ticket to China was the last thing I wanted.

The eunuch continued to kiss and fondle me. Not knowing about the biological quirk as a result of which I was perpetually erect, he evidently had assumed that my stiffness was the result of his ministrations. Grunting happily, he began making warm, wet circles on my flesh with

59

his tongue. I shuddered, and to take my mind off what he was doing, I turned my attentions to the pygmy girl with the full, round breasts.

She was still sitting cross-legged at the edge of the tub, her *sitar* cradled in her lap, her nasal chant moving in weird counterpoint to the instrument's exotic melody. My eyes zeroed in on her breasts, which rose and fell rhythmically as she sang. I imagined myself in bed with her, my mouth closed over one of the breasts, my hand gently stroking the other. Even without the hashish, the thought would have been a groovy one. With the hashish, it was dynamite.

I let my imagination run a little farther. As the scene played itself out, my fingers deftly unfastened the cord which held her pantaloons around her waist. Then I quickly slipped the garment over her hips and down her thighs, exposing a glistening expanse of exciting black skin. My lips worked their way over her trim, flat belly, while my palm stroked her bare thighs. Then I positioned her beneath me and launched my invasion.

The feeling was great. Too great. And I suddenly realized why. It wasn't entirely imaginary. The eunuch, keeping pace with my reverie, had begun to gratify me orally.

Wincing with disgust, I turned to Douzi. He was leaning back on the bench, his tiny legs spread wide, his childlike face a portrait of ecstasy as his eunuch performed on him the same exercise which my eunuch was performing on me. "Isn't it marvelous, Damon?" he grinned when he noticed that I was looking at him. "Doesn't it really excite you?"

I swallowed hard. "Frankly, it leaves me cold."

His expression testified to his disappointment. "Damon, I'm afraid I overestimated you. I thought you were a genuine libertine, but now I find that you're—what's the American expression?—a square."

"All things have their season," I quipped. "And this is my season for girls."

He shrugged, like a host who has just served *filet mignon a la béarnaise* only to find that his guest prefers hamburgers with ketchup.

"Ah, Damon," he said, "you have no taste whatsoever."

60

Then, forcing a smile, he added, "But this is your welcoming party, so we'll do things your way." He clapped his hands. "On with the girls."

The two eunuchs vanished through the door leading to the *tepidarium*, and the two pygmy men with the pipes promptly returned to the bench where Douzi and I were sitting. I was still feeling the effects of the last round of hash, so I made it a point to draw very lightly on my pipe and to exhale the smoke as soon as I had inhaled it. But Douzi apparently was determined to smoke himself right up into the stratosphere. He puffed even more enthusiastically than before, and when he exhaled only the faintest traces of smoke seeped out of his nostrils.

A minute passed, then another. Finally Douzi looked up from his pipe and gestured toward the door. "The girls, Damon," he beamed proudly. "What do you think of them?"

I didn't answer right away. I couldn't—because I was dumbstruck.

Back in the States, when Walrus-moustache told me that I'd be playing stud to a stable of female physicists, I had assumed that the dolls would be at least bearable and at worst uglier than sin. To my utter amazement all nine were far better than bearable and two or three were raving beauties.

The first girl to enter the room was a tall, statuesque brunette with warm brown eyes and breasts that were too perfect to be anything but really real. She wore a multicolored silk kimono that was held in place only by a thin black cincture knotted loosely around her waist. Through the kimono's open front I got a glimpse of the inner slopes of her bountiful breasts. The massive mammaries were enough to warm the heart of even a jaded old Coxeman like me.

Her escort was a slender black-skinned eunuch who wore loose-fitting pink silk pantaloons and a matching turban. He led her on his arm around the marble tub to one of the stools at a corner wall fountain. She eyed me interestedly as she passed my bench, then lowered hereslf gingerly into her seat and stretched her sexy legs in front of her. The eunuch dutifully sat on the floor next to her and began gently kissing her thighs.

Next came a medium-sized cutie in a hopsack mini-robe that hung just an inch or two below the underslope of her buttocks. Her raven black hair was short and fell around her ears in a coiffure reminiscent of Prince Valiant. Her eyes were a sexy ice blue, her lips were moist and hot pink, and her bare legs were exciting enough to take my mind off her other endowments—at least for a while.

She was escorted by a eunuch who was even bigger than the hefty duo who had undressed Douzi and me. Like the first girl's eunuch, he wore pink silk pantaloons and a matching turban. He led his pretty mate along the path the first couple had followed, then sat on the floor alongside her and reached under her robe to stroke her buttocks with one hand while he cradled her legs across his lap with the other.

The third girl was an Oriental who wore a gauze-thin, floor-length nightgown. Beneath the sheer fabric I could see the enticing form of her pert, tiny breasts and smooth, generously curved hips. Her movements were a symphony of sensuality.

She accompanied her pink-pantalooned eunuch around the tub to the cluster of stools where the other girls were sitting, then tucked her legs underneath her fanny and smiled at me provocatively. My eyes fixed appreciatively to the soft features of her pretty face—the gentle, almond-shaped eyes, the tiny button-nose, the tender, little-girl's mouth with its two rows of perfectly even pearl-white teeth. The eunuch draped an arm around her sexy hips and pressed his face lovingly against her belly.

Next came another Caucasian girl, a tall blonde in a mini-nightie that revealed far more than it concealed. She was followed by a sloe-eyed brunette in a knee-length kimono; her body was the stuff that turned dreams wet. Then came another Oriental cutie, a petite charmer whose delicate features begged for gentle and loving caresses. Then a third Oriental girl, small-boned but amply fleshed, with full round breasts and a set of hips that just wouldn't quit. Next another Caucasian—medium tall, with long brown hair and as sexy a pair of legs as ever walked. She was flat-chested, but still very sexy. Last came another tall blonde, more beautiful than any of her predecessors, and almost if not quite as sensational in the body department.

I waited until all nine of the lovelies were seated with their pink-pantalooned eunuchs. Then I turned to Douzi. "Well," I said dryly, "no doubt about it, these chicks are real knockouts. But where are the nine I'm supposed to entertain?"

The joke went over his head. "Where are they?" he echoed incredulously. "Why, they're here. These are they."

"You're kidding," I kidded. "Why, these dolls are—" I stopped short. I had almost said that these dolls were twenty-four-karat sexbombs, and whoever heard of a female physicist being sexy? But I remembered just in time that Douzi wasn't supposed to know that I knew the chicks were physicists. Promising myself to be a lot more careful about slips of the tongue from now on, I hastily amended, "These dolls don't need a stud service. They could get any man they wanted on their own."

Douzi smiled beningly. "Let me decide what they need, Damon. Your job is to entertain them, and if you find them attractive, so much the better, because it'll make your work easier."

"I expect," I admitted, "that it'll be the easiest job in my career." To myself, I added, "At least until I start asking where the bombs are stored."

Douzi's right arm made a sweeping gesture that took in all nine girls. "You'll notice," he commented, "that each of them has her own eunuch. These eunuchs function as their servants. They make the girls' beds, clean their rooms, run errands for them, and in general cater to their whims and act as protectors."

My eyes fixed on the eunuch with the raven-haired doll in the hopsack minirobe. He sat cross-legged between her knees, his fingers gingerly massaging her bare buttocks while his tongue probed hungrily between her thighs. "Including sexual whims?" I asked, nodding toward the couple.

Douzi's eyes followed my gaze. He chuckled softly. "In-
63

sofar as is possible. Naturally there are limits to what a eunuch can do—especially since all these eunuchs are, like the two who undressed us, cleanly amputated. Also, for reasons of my own, I do not permit these eunuchs to kiss the girls on the mouth or elsewhere above the neck. However, apart from this limitation and those imposed by the eunuchs' characteristic deformity, the relationship is one of anything goes—provided, of course, that the girl wants it."

"And my job is to take up where the eunuchs leave off?"

"Precisely. I can see that you're admirably suited to the task." He nodded toward my ever-erect manhood. "Also, you like the girls. So there should be no problems."

"What about Superman?"

His eyebrows arched quizzically. "You know about him?"

I gulped, realizing that I'd just made another slip. "Su Wing mentioned earlier that he was here," I ad-libbed. "She said he was having trouble keeping all the girls happy."

"Well, let's just say that two heads are better than one. That's why I welcomed you here. I expect that you and Superman together will keep the girls a lot happier than either of you would single-handedly. And I can't make the point too strongly, Damon: the girls must be kept happy."

"Why?" I prodded, hoping to get him talking along lines that would be interesting to The Coxe Foundation back in the states.

He grinned, as if to say that he realized I was baiting him and that he wouldn't fall for it. "Because I say so," he said after a moment. "Isn't that reason enough?"

"It's reason enough," I mumbled. But inwardly I was seething. I've always been the type of guy who likes to know the "why" of everything. I even wanted to know the "why" back when I was in the Army where they're not obliged to tell you. Now, in less than forty-eight hours, I'd turned myself over to a pair of commanders—Douzi and Lin Saong—who not only refused to tell the "why" but often were mysterious about even the "who," "what," "when," "where" and "how." It was enough to make an old-line Indian like me sincerely wish he could be a chief for once.

But I didn't dwell on the matter too long. And for a very good reason. The reason was Su Wing.

No sooner had Douzi and I finished our little exchange than she came tripping into the room on the arm of her eunuch. She wore a tentlike black leather shift, the hem of which barely covered her Golden Treasure. With each step of her small, shapely legs the hem flopped upward, and more than once I was sure I had glimpsed the lovely down which feathered her nest.

Douzi stood as she approached the bench, and I followed suit. She bowed politely to me, then snuggled up against Douzi's side. Earlier, during my tour with her around the palace grounds, I'd been impressed by her smallness. Now, standing next to the diminutive Douzi, she looked like an amazon.

My eyes darted over the smooth expanse of her bare legs, the legs which a couple hours earlier had been wrapped hungrily around mine. I was really anxious to have another go-round with her.

But, with the situation being what it was, thoughts like that could only get me into trouble. I forced myself to look away from her and to concentrate on what was happening with the nine physicists and their eunuchs.

A lot was happening. The buxom brunette with the bountiful breasts had shucked her kimono and was having both her nippled treasures worked over at the same time; the eunuch who had escorted her into the room was licking away at one, while the eunuch of the Oriental next to her was lapping the other.

The Oriental herself had taken up with one of the two eunuchs who had undressed Douzi and me. The black giant was sitting on her stool with her on his lap and facing away from him; each of his hands was frantically gyrating one of her breasts while his enormous mouth nibbled lustfully at her neck. Meanwhile, the doll in the hopsack mini-robe had carried her little brand of self-amusement to its logical conclusion; her legs were wrapped around her eunuch's neck while his face was buried deeply in her crotch; the ecstatic expression on her face suggested that if she wasn't experiencing orgasm she was damned close to it.

"In a few minutes," Douzi said, interrupting my concentration on the spectacle, "Superman will be here and the show will begin. Su Wing will sit with me during the performance, and, of course, we'll make love. If you'd like a girl to sit with you, you may take your pick from among the nine—and you may have her eunuch with her, if you choose."

I wasn't too turned on about the eunuch angle. But the idea of having one of the nine girls was right up my alley. Less than four hours had passed since my double-header in the car with Su Wing. But the sight of the nine lovelies—so primed up for sex that they were now going at it hot and heavy with their eunuchs—really set my motor running.

I wondered which one to pick.

The brunette interested me. I've always been something of a breast-man, and her set was as exciting as any I'd ever come across.

The cutie in the hopsack mini-robe did great things for me also. If she could manage to get all worked up over a little tonguing by a eunuch, I could imagine how wild she'd be while being pleasured by The Real Thing.

Then there was the small-boned Oriental girl with the hips that wouldn't quit. Since coming to Belgravia I'd been on a strictly Far East diet, and the cuisine was very much to my liking.

And there was the tall blonde who entered the room last. If she was as good in a clinch as she was in the looks department, she'd be woman enough to satisfy any man.

But I had other things to think of besides my own preferences. I realized that the success of my mission depended on how quickly I could get one of the nine dolls to open up about the location of the bombs. That meant that my best move would be to pick the one chick who'd be most likely to need my loving—the oldest and ugliest in the lot.

Actually none of the chicks was really ugly, and the oldest couldn't have been more than thirty-five, but as I surveyed the nine of them, I got the impression that one, the medium-tall Caucasian with the long brown hair and the super-sexy legs, was a little less happy with the whole situation than were her eight colleagues. While all the others were frolicking eagerly with their eunuchs, she was sitting very sedately on her stool, her eyes staring off into the distance, her expression one of total boredom.

I tried to imagine how she would fit into my scheme of things if I had come to the harem as Superman had—not seeking information, but just looking to earn my salary of a thousand dollars a week. Probably, I told myself, I'd give all the broads a quick shot, starting with the brunette with the big jugs and continuing down the line until I'd finally hit all nine. Then I'd pick the three or four chicks who pleased me most, and I'd make them my favorites, servicing all the others only often enough to keep boss-man Douzi from getting on my back about being negligent.

Yep, that was the way I'd do it, and unless I missed my guess, that was the way Superman had done it. Which meant that five or six of the dolls were now as frustrated as all get-out. And from what I could see, the babe with the long brown hair and the super-sexy legs was the most frustrated of the batch.

"I'll take that one," I told Douzi, pointing at her.

He looked up from Su Wing's leather shift, the bodice of which he had been gnawing on hungrily. "She's yours," he said quickly. Then, barking something in Belgravian at a nearby eunuch, he resumed gnawing on the dress. I wondered idly if there was any sexual quirk which my half-pint host *didn't* subscribe to. It's not very often that you come across a guy who grooves on eunuchs' deformities, who digs homosexual fellatio and who's a leather fetishist to boot—even if sex *is* your business.

The eunuch scurried across the room, said something to the chick I had picked, then brought her and her eunuch to me. She seemed surprised that I wanted her, probably self-conscious of her small-bosom, but she didn't seem at all unhappy about it. I gave her a warm, welcoming hug. "Hi," I said. "My name's Damon, what's yours?"

She blushed, and the corners of her pretty mouth turned

67

upward in a small smile. But she said nothing.

"Don't be shy," I coaxed. "I'm not going to hurt you. President Douzi brought me here to entertain you. So, like they say on Broadway, "*Let Me Entertain You, Let Me Make You Smile . . .*"

No dice. She blushed again, and her smile broadened. But she still wouldn't say a word.

I wondered idly if it was my charm that was wearing out or just my twenty-four-hour deodorant. "Don't you like me?" I asked. "If you don't, I won't bother you . . ."

Her eunuch muttered something in Belgravian to my eunuch, and my eunuch conveyed the message to Douzi. "Her name," said he, "is Olga. And she doesn't speak a word of English."

I sighed. Ninety per cent of the scientific community the world over speaks English, and I had to pick a chick from the ten per cent that doesn't. Fat chance of getting her to tell me where the bombs were hidden!

But I'd made my selection and it was too late now to change my mind, especially if I didn't want to arouse Douzi's suspicions. "Oh, well," I told him, "the language of love is universal. I'm sure we'll get along." Then, taking her by the hand, I retreated to the bench at the opposite side of the tub.

Once we were seated it didn't take her long to warm up to me. I put my arm around her shoulders, and she snuggled cuddlesomely against my chest. I kissed her lightly on the cheek and she obligingly offered me her mouth. I thrust my tongue inside, and she began sucking on it hungrily. Then I brought my hand to her thighs, and they parted eagerly.

"Olga," I said softly, "you're beautiful." Remembering the language barrier, I tried translating the thought into French. Then into German. Then into Spanish. Then into Italian.

No luck. The bewildered expression on her face told me that, while she might be a real hotshot at nuclear physics, she was strictly nowhere when it came to European languages.

Some years before, when I was killing a quiet summer on

campus at my university, I'd become interested in a chick who was enrolled in a Russian class. To get to meet her, I'd enrolled in the class. After four sessions, I'd got where I wanted to get with her and I'd dropped the course. Now, wracking my brain to remember a few of the words I'd learned before dropping out, I said in Russian what I hoped she'd understand as "What languages do you speak?"

She replied in a torrent of words which mystified me completely. My linguistic shot-in-the-dark might've been right on target, but even if I had hit the bull's-eye, I had no way of knowing it.

Dipping back into my memories of that Russian class, I came up with some words I hoped she'd understand as, "Forget it." Then, abandoning all attempts at verbal communication, I settled back to enjoy what we had going for us on a physical plane.

It was a lot. Her long, shapely legs were twin pillars of pulchritude that sent my desire skyrocketing into the stratosphere. I gently stroked her thighs, then inched my hand upward until it had come to rest against the throbbing wet well of her womanhood. Her hips slid forward on the bench, and the hot juices of her passion inundated me. I parted the lips of her nether-mouth, and my finger found its way inside.

She began squirming delightedly. Her hand closed around my ever-ready saber, and her wrist took up a brisk traversing motion. At the same time her mouth found mine, and her tongue flickered frantically across my teeth.

No doubt about it, we were really communicating physically. Now if I could just figure out a way to break the verbal language barrier.

But how?

CHAPTER FIVE

I was still wondering when a ripple of excitement surged through the room and I looked up to be greeted by the spectacle that was Superman's grand entrance.

Grand?

That's an understatement.

Emperor Constantine returning to Rome in A.D. 33 after sacking Byzantium couldn't have done things up more ceremoniously.

The first member of the conquering super-stud's retinue to enter the room was a bare-breasted pygmy girl swinging a golden censer. She paused before Douzi's bench and bowed, then positioned herself at one end of the marble tub and ritualistically shot a waft of sweet-smelling smoke toward each of the nine physicists and her eunuch-companion.

Next came two male pygmy censer-bearers. They stationed themselves at right angles to the girl, and the three of them began swinging their censers vigorously toward the center of the tub. In seconds the room was thick with smoke, and the overpowering aroma of incense pervaded the air completely.

Following the two male pygmies was a giant eunuch decked out in green silk. He carried a gold tray, on which was a purple velvet pillow, and on which was a clear plastic dome. I couldn't see what was under the dome, but having become familiar with the "fountain of youth" via my sexual studies, I had a pretty good idea of what it was—a fly, a common, ordinary housefly the wings of which had been amputated.

The eunuch was followed by two more male pygmies,

who carried small basins filled with a colorless liquid. Then came two female pygmies, carrying wooden salad bowls laden with exotic-looking herbs. The quartet positioned themselves between the three censer-bearers, and on a signal from the eunuch, dropped to their knees.

A few seconds passed, then a few more. Then, after Douzi sharply clapped his hands, the star of the show made his appearance.

I looked.

And I looked again.

Then I looked a third time.

I recalled Walrus-moustache's appraisal of my competitor's phallic endowments: "He's hung, buddy. Really hung."

Then I recalled a line from the *Satyricon* of Petronius: " 'Tis uncertain whether the organ's an appendage of the man, or the man of the organ."

Looking at Superman I had no doubts as to what was appended to whom. But I sure as hell wondered how he managed to walk upright with an extra foot—at least!

And he wasn't the least bit reticent about displaying his charms. He wore only a white, floor-length cape fastened around his shoulders by a thin silver chain and open at the front in such a manner that his bountiful truncheon was openly displayed.

I remembered that I had told Walrus-moustache that it's not what you have but the way that you use it. All I could say now was that I'd better use what I had pretty damned skillfully.

As a second pair of bare-breasted pygmy girls followed him with smoke-spouting censers, my nemesis strode majestically to the center of the marble tub. Head haughtily held high, shoulders proudly thrust back, he turned a small right-face toward Douzi. Then, executing a small and almost condescending bow, he did an about-face toward me. His bow this time was accompanied by a sneer, which I returned. Then he right-faced toward the femme physicists, whom he favored with individual bows and smiles before about-facing again toward the door.

These maneuvers having been completed, a eunuch

71

materialized behind him and took his cape. Then he lay on his back in the tub, his head resting on a pillow at the tub's edge.

Promptly the five pygmy girls in his retinue positioned themselves on all fours around him. One, kneeling over his face, dangled her breasts provocatively in front of his mouth; he began licking them hungrily. Two others coiled their bodies snake-like over his outstretched arms and began kissing him wetly on both sides of the neck while his fingers dived under the waistbands of their pantaloons and went to work on their Jade Treasures. The final two coiled around his legs and began kissing and licking his mammoth member, which promptly shot up to a high present-arms.

I glanced across the room at Douzi, who obviously was enjoying the spectacle immensely. Since I last had looked at him, he had managed to hike Su Wing's leather shift up above her waist and to maneuver her into place on her back across the bench. Now he sat locked in sexual combat with her, his legs straddling the bench, her legs wrapped around his waist, while he looked over his shoulder at Superman's performance. His tiny body was taut with excitement, and his eyes were bulging like a pair of forty-two-D breasts squeezed into a thirty-six-C bra.

My physicist companion, Olga, evidently was enjoying the spectacle also. During Superman's grand entrance, she had managed to slide one leg over my lap and to line up my Stalwart Stallion with her Precious Sheath. During his de-caping routine, she had managed to impale herself neatly on it. Now, as I peered over her shoulder at Superman and his five handmaidens, she was jouncing around on me like a cowgirl astride a bucking bronco.

Gyrating my hips in a sensuous counter-rhythm to her movements, I continued to watch the show. After a moment, Douzi clapped his hands, and one of the eunuchs turned on a water fountain. The pygmy girls scurried out of the tub as the water began trickling into it. When Superman was submerged completely except for his face and his still-stiff staff, Douzi clapped his hands a second time. The fountain then was turned off and the eunuch with the dome-covered velvet pillow waded into the tub.

72

The time now had come for the "fountain of youth," and, as I watched the eunuch remove the dome from the pillow," I wondered if Superman's version of the ritual would be the same as that which had been practiced in nineteenth century Paris whorehouses after the invasion by alumnae of the Constantinople harem of Abd ul-Hamid II.

I had ample reason to wonder. In the Paris version, the name "fountain of youth" was especially appropriate, because the person who would serve as the "fountain" inevitably was an adolescent boy. Once he had been brought to erection, the fly with the amputated wings would be placed on the tip of his penis. Then the fly would continue to walk around until its movements brought the boy to orgasm.

The reason a boy was used for the ceremony rather than a man was because a boy's penis is far more sensitive than a man's. Most men would need twenty to thirty minutes or longer to be aroused by the fly to the point where they would ejaculate, and many would lose their erection before ejaculation could take place. A boy, on the other hand, could be stimulated to orgasm in five minutes or less.

Superman was no boy. In fact, he was thirty-five years old if he was a day. I found it hard to believe that his reflexes would be quick enough to permit him to perform the "fountain of youth" as it originally was intended to be performed.

The eunuch who was attending him took the fly from beneath the dome and placed it carefully on his penis. The immense organ vibrated wildly as the tiny insect began to walk around it. Then it stood perfectly still, and only the grotesque contortions of Superman's rugged sun-bronzed face served as testimony to the erogenous efficacy of the fly's movements.

Across the room, Douzi was gaping like a kid at his first peep-show. The half-pint President still was coitally joined to Su Wing, and his tiny hips continued to hammer against her. But his eyes were riveted to Superman's shaft and the wingless fly that was crawling atop it.

The femme physicists were getting quite a bang out of the ceremony, too. The blonde with the bountiful bosom

73

had her two eunuchs working double-time on her breasts, while with one hand she was vigorously massaging her most intimate areas. The Oriental cutie next to her was doing some massaging also. And the raven-haired doll in the hopsack minirobe had grabbed her eunuch by the ears and was pressing his face so hard against her most erogenous zone that I thought for sure she was going to break his nose.

A few minutes passed. The fly continued to walk its post, and Superman continued to grimace in response to its stimulation, but the moment everyone was waiting for seemed nowhere in sight.

That is, Superman's moment was nowhere in sight. Olga's moment suddenly was closer than close.

Her hips began grinding double-time, and her fingernails dug ferociously into the tensed muscles of my thighs. I thrust harder against her. She tossed back her head and bit fiercely into my neck. My palms cupped her breasts, and I began gyrating them wildly. Then her body stiffened. She moaned something in Russian which I couldn't translate. But I had no trouble getting the message. I had just taken her where she wanted to go.

I waited until the last spasm of sensation had left her. Then I slowly resumed my thrusting. She seemed kind of surprised that I wasn't ready to drop out of the race. But she wasn't at all unhappy about it. Murmuring sexily, she adjusted the rhythm of her hip movements to match mine. I kissed her on the cheeck and went to work in earnest, resolved that this turn around I'd show her an even better time than the first.

Out in the tub, Superman's grimaces were becoming more intense. His audience evidnetly knew this to be a sign that the fountain was about to spurt, because all of the girls began watching him more closely. Douzi was watching closely too, and to make sure I didn't miss The Big Moment, he began waving at me frantically.

I watched, and I saw what I hadn't expected to see. Superman might've been well into his thirties, but he performed the "fountain of youth" as flawlessly as the nineteenth century's most youthful Parisian might've

74

performed it. There was a brief, expectant moment during which his proud pike quivered wildly. Then, like Old Faithful, the geyser erupted. All told, the enterprise had taken less than ten minutes. Competitiveness aside, I couldn't help but applaud the performance.

The ceremony now over, Douzi waded into the tub and patted his champion on the back. Then he brought him to my bench, and we were introduced formally.

"Pleased to meet you—and mighty impressed with your talent," I said amiably, shaking his hand.

He dismissed the compliment with a superior shrug. "It's all in a day's work."

"Speaking of work," Douzi put in, "I can think of no better time than the present to see both of you in action. You, Damon, have already entertained Olga. But the other eight girls remain unsatisfied. I'm going to divide them into two groups of four each—one group for you and one for Superman. I'll have the eunuchs turn on the steam. Then you can do your love-making right here in the tub. It should be an interesting situation for all concerned. You'll be making love under water, and in a room as hot as any steam bath."

"Actually," I interrupted, "I haven't quite finished with Olga yet." And I hadn't. Superman's eruption had cut short our second round just when it was starting to get good.

But Douzi wasn't about to have his plans upset. "She had her chance," he said. "Now the other girls must have theirs."

He said something in Belgravian to one of the eunuchs, and the steam was turned on. Then he said something else, and the girls were divided into two groups. I was assigned the tall blonde with the beautiful face, the sloe-eyed brunette with the wild body, the Oriental girl with the fantastic hips and the statuesque brunette with the bountiful boobs.

Superman took his girls to one side of the tub, and I took mine to the other. Then we got down to business.

I tackled the sloe-eyed brunette first. Her name was Nadia, and she evidently had been very favorably impressed by my jousting wth Olga, because she came running at me

75

with open arms. I would've liked to have set the stage with some long-drawn-out foreplay, but Douzi wasn't in the mood for delays and I wasn't in the mood to haggle with him. So, flipping her onto her back in hot water, I silently launched my invasion. A few minute later her moans and groans told me that I'd given her what she wanted to get.

Through the corner of my eye I could see that Superman was still going at it hot and heavy with his Number One cutie, so I kept Nadia in place beneath me. She was pleasantly surprised to learn that she had a double-feature going for her, and she rewarded me by hipping up one of the wildest sex-storms I'd ever experienced. It wasn't long before I was at the edge of the ledge myself.

But I didn't let myself go off. I knew that my success with the nine femmes would depend on showing them that I was a better man than Superman, and I had to make sure they read the message loud and clear. Biting my lip to take my mind off the maddening passions that were bubbling down below, I continued to hammer away. Nadia matched me stroke for stroke, each stroke making it harder for me to hold back.

Finally Superman's chick skyrocketed off into sex-tasyville, and he shoved her out roughly from underneath him. Playing the game for all it was worth, I slowed my rhythm to a leisurely larghetto and increased the depth and force of my thrusts. The change of pace made Nadia go wild with desire. In less than a minute she was up-up-and-away. Happily I stopped biting my lip and soared right up there with her.

"Dr. Damon," she smiled, staggering to her feet, "you're too much."

"Thanks," I murmured, pecking her lightly on the cheek. "But why didn't you tell me you spoke English?"

Her smile went coquettish. "You didn't ask."

It was my turn to smile. "Well, we'll have lots to talk about from now on."

Her eyes made a quick, appreciative tour of my body. "Yes," she said. "Lots and lots and lots."

She retreated to the marble stool where her eunuch was

waiting for her, and the second girl in my fabulous foursome took her place. It was the Oriental girl with the marvelous hips.

Smiling amiably, I fell back on my old line. "Hi, my name's Damon, what's yours?" I said.

She looked at me evenly. "I am sorry," she said in perfectly unaccented English, "but I do not speak English. This is the only English sentence I know."

I did a double take. "You've got to be kidding."

"I am sorry," she repeated, "but I do not speak English. This is the only English sentence I know."

I didn't know whether she was putting me on or not. But I decided I'd have plenty of time to check her linguistic talents later. Superman had already flopped down with his second cutie, and I didn't want to fall too far behind. Maneuvering the hippy honey into place beneath me, I went back to work.

I had wanted to give her, like Nadia, two orgasms for the price of one. But I couldn't quite make it. Her super-sexy gyrations were just more than I could handle.

I tried distracting myself by biting my lip, then by biting my tongue. Then I tried counting backwards from ninety-nine to one. Then I attempted to list all the major U.S. foreign policy errors from the end of World War II to the present.

The distractions worked for a while. But just as she was coasting down from her peak, I found myself scooting up toward mine. I kept thrusting after I got there, but she unexplainably stopped. Our language barrier made it impossible for me to tell her that I wasn't through with her yet, and I could only assume that she sensed that I had had orgasm and that she believed once a chick was enough for any guy.

Whatever the case, she slid out from beneath me and returned to her eunuch. I told myself that perhaps it was just as well. My manhood was still as capable as ever, but my back was sure as hell getting sore.

At this point Superman took a break. He sat on the edge of the tub, his feet dangling in the water, and summoned one of the pygmy girls from his retinue. She hurried to him, carrying the wooden salad bowl laden with exotic-looking herbs, which she had brought into the room during the original procession. She was followed by one of the pygmy men carrying a small basin filled with a colorless liquid.

I decided to take a break myself. Ambling over next to him, I plopped down on the edge of the tub and curiously regarded the contents of the salad bowl, which he was shoveling into his mouth with great gusto. "What's up, Doc?" I asked. "A little Vitamin E for sustenance?"

"A little mountain greenery," he growled back between mouthfuls. "Just for the hell of it."

Douzi materialized behind us. "Actually, Damon, Superman's eating a rare Belgravian plant called the *khourba*. The girls have been fed on it. It has remarkable aphrodisiacal qualities. I've just eaten some myself, and you can see the results."

I turned to face him. Sure enough, the *khourba* had worked. His rifle was at a proud port-arms.

But it really didn't have anything to be proud about. According to an old wives' tale among sexologists, pygmies are supposed to be tiny in every detail except penis growth—which is supposed to be comparable to the penis growth of full-sized males. But Douzi—and I was surprised at myself for not having noticed it before—was as small in the penis department as he was everywhere else. Little wonder that Su Wing went ga-ga over me in the car if she had nothing but *his* modest merchandise to keep her happy before I arrived.

"There's some *khourka* here for you too, Damon, if you'd like some," Douzi went on. Then, glancing at my groin, he added quickly, "But you seem to be doing quite well without it." His eyes widened in admiration. "How do you manage to stay rigid for so long?"

I saw no point in cluing him in just yet on the secret to my insatiable virility. "Lets just say that this is one of my good days. If I need any *khourba*, I'll let you know."

Douzi returned to his bench, and Superman finished his bowl of *khourba*. "If there's anything I hate, Damon," the abundantly endowed—but now very limp—super-stud told me, "it's a show-off."

I grinned amiably. "Like talk about pots calling kettles black."

His brow furrowed. "The American slang—I don't understand it."

"You will, champ," I chuckled. "Just give me time."

He evidently decided to quit our little verbal duel before he fell even farther behind. Turning away from me, he lay on his back along the edge of the tub. Then he snapped his fingers and the pygmy man with the basin of colorless liquid knelt beside him.

The liquid, I noticed, smelled something like rubbing alcohol. But I had a sneaking suspicion that it was a lot more than just that. I recalled reading during the course of my sexual studies that the ancient Hindus favored aphrodisiacal potions which were massaged into the genitalia rather than being consumed internally, as is the case with most aphrodisiacs.

A favorite such potion, described in *The Perfumed Garden* by Sheikh Nefzawi, is made from pieces of arris root mixed with mango oil. Once the mixture has been prepared, it's stored for six months in an aperture in the trunk of a situ tree. The ointment which then is extracted from the aperture is applied manually, and is supposed to be very effective.

I was willing to bet that the liquid in Superman's basin was something of this sort, probably something Douzi had cooked up using Belgravian equivalents of the Indian raw materials.

The pygmy basin-bearer carefully stirred his compound, then touched a drop of it to his arm. Evidently satisfied that the preparation was okay, he summoned the pygmy girl who had brought Superman the *khourba*. She promptly dipped a cloth into the basin and began scrubbing the supine warrior's wherewithals.

I might not have needed anything aphrodisiacal, but the idea of having one of the tiny girls scrub me was suddenly very interesting. I told Douzi what I had in mind and he

79

obligingly summoned another basinful of the stuff. Lying on my back, I closed my eyes and waited for my pygmy girl to go to work.

I didn't have to wait long, and I didn't need to look to realize that the scrubbing had begun. No sooner had the liquid-soaked washcloth been touched to my groin than my whole torso screamed out with pain. I felt like I was being broiled, boiled, roasted and fried—all at once. A thousand fiery tongues shot through my flesh, and an uncontrollable spasm contracted the muscles in my lower abdomen.

"Hey!" I heard myself shout. "What is this stuff? Liquid lightning?"

"It's one of my private preparations," smiled Douzi, standing over me and watching with interest as my pygmy girl vigorously massaged me with her washcloth. "It'll smart for a while, but the sting won't last long. And when it goes, you'll have nothing but pleasure."

He was as good as his word. The stuff burned fiercely for about a minute and a half, then the burning slowly subsided and a warm glow took its place—a glow that felt very much like the sensation just before orgasm. Only this glow was better, because it didn't stop.

My pygmy girl watched me writhe and squirm under the love potion's influence. Then, dropping her washcloth in the basin, she leaned over me and began to kiss the area which she had just bathed.

Her lips were soft and super-sensuous. Her tongue was hot and wet and oh-so-talented. The warm glow which the aphrodisiac had triggered inside me grew hotter. Still, release was nowhere in sight.

The girl's tight, round mouth closed around my manhood, and her head began moving gingerly up and down. Her tiny teeth nibbled at me teasingly, and her tongue was flickering a mile-a-minute. The sensation built, and it built some more. But I still wasn't close to climaxing.

"I think he's ready, Dr. Douzi," said a sexily British accented voice behind me. "And frankly so am I." To me she said, "What do you think, Damon? Shall we have a go at it?"

80

I looked up at a pair of classically proportioned breasts that were dangling provocatively over my face. Peering over them was the statuesque brunette who had led the original parade into the room.

Douzi was standing next to her, beaming at me like a fastidious *maître d'hotel* regarding his chef's most celebrated *pièce de résistance*. "You heard her," he rasped in a football-coach voice. "She's ready. So give her what she wants."

Suppressing my resentment of his master-to-slave manner, I gently disengaged myself from the caresses of the pretty and ultra-talented pygmy girl. Then I ushered my new customer into the pool.

"My first name's Vera," she told me en route. "What's yours?"

"Rod," I replied.

"Rod?" She giggled lasciviously. "How appropriate."

I smiled to myself. Not that the pun was original or anything like that, but it was nice to know that my chick was fluent enough in English to use the kind of idioms they generally don't teach in language courses. I didn't know what kind of sexual shenanigans it would take to win her over to my side, but if I did win her over, I'd have no trouble understanding the information she gave me.

When we were in the water, she automatically flopped over on her back and spread her legs. The thought of her breasts pressing against my chest while we made love was very appealing. But the thought of kneading them with my hands while I entered her from behind was even more appealing.

"Turn over, baby," I said, giving her a playful pinch. "We're going to make this one doggie-style."

She evidently liked the idea. Clutching my eagerly distended manhood for support, she got up and turned toward the edge of the tub. Then, leaning against the edge, she offered me her buttocks.

By this time the steam which the eunuchs had turned on earlier was so thick I could hardly see her, but I didn't mind. It was fun feeling my way.

81

My hands groped around until they were clutching her firm, neatly rounded buttocks. Then they slid over her hips and down her thighs. I parted her thighs, and kneeling behind her, I maneuvered my sex into place. Then I pushed forward.

She jumped as I entered her swiftly. "Oh!" she squealed. "That feels so good!"

It felt good to me too. In fact, it felt very good. The hot, tight pressure of the velvety-smooth walls inside her reawakened the warm glow which the pygmy girl's scrubbing had set off. My body suddenly was as taut as a violin string, and great shock waves of sensation surged through me—sensation that built and built until every cell of my being was alive with it.

Leaning forward, I took her breasts in my hands. They were full and round and unbelievably firm. I squeezed them tightly, and she shuddered with pleasure. Then I began gyrating them. Her hips set off at a frantic gallop. I licked the base of her neck.

The sensation inside me continued to build. I pumped harder, and it built some more. My legs were trembling, and I was gasping for breath. But I kept on pumping away, and the sensation kept building higher and higher and higher until I thought the top of my head was going to blow off.

"Oh, Rod! Ohh, ohhhh, Rodddd!!!" Vera was screaming. "Oh, Rod, you're so hard! And so strong! And so powerful!"

I didn't know whether she was addressing me or my manhood, but I liked what I was hearing, so I didn't let up.

"Rod!" she went on. "You don't know how good this feels! Oh, it's so wonderful! And, Damon, your hands feel so good, too! Keep doing what you're doing with them! Please don't stop! It's so good! And I'm going to—I'm going to—"

Well, one thing was clear anyway. I might not have been the Rod she was talking to the first time, but she sure as hell was talking to me now, not only with words, but also with the unbelievably wild movements of her overcharged hips.

Gritting my teeth to keep the ever-building sensation from running away with me completely, I hammered against her all the harder.

"Oh!" she gasped. "Ohhhhh!"

Her orgasm was like the chain detonation of all the gunpowder in an ammo dump. First there were a few little blasts. Then one or two slightly bigger ones. Then a really big one. Then a bigger one still. Then two that were absolutely stupendous. Then two that were only moderately big. Then a series of little ones that finally ended in something of mere firecracker dimensions.

With each blast, her body convulsed wildly—and the convulsions were always proportionate to the strength of the blast. In response to the two stupendous jolts in the middle she shook so violently that she almost knocked me out of the saddle.

I'd've liked to think that it was nothing but my sexmanship which was producing this reaction in her. But I had a feeling that Douzi's aphrodisiac lotion also had something to do with it too. Perhaps, I reasoned, the lotion, having penetrated my skin, had during coitus, managed to penetrate her skin also.

Whatever the case, our joust had certainly given her a king-size jolt. And I apparently had an even better one in store for me when I finally hit the top. I redoubled my efforts.

Somewhere to my right I could hear Superman splashing around in the water with the third doll in his foursome. From what I could hear of their conversation, I got the impression that they were just starting what Vera and I had already finished. That meant I had more time to work with than I originally had reckoned on. I slowed the pace of my thrusting, determined that this time around I'd give Vera a shot she'd really remember.

She matched her rhythm to mine. At the same time, her face swiveled around and her tongue went to work on the side of my neck. I tightened my grip on her breasts, and thrust-wise kept a steady course.

I was still keeping the course a few minutes later when the gasps and groans of Superman's sexmate heralded her plunge into passionsville. Promptly picking up my thrust-tempo, I sent Vera off on her second orbit of the afternoon.

And what an orbit it was! She squealed like a stuck pig, and her hips began gyrating like the agitator on a brand spankin' new automatic washer. Then the explosions started again, and this time they were twice as intense and twice as numerous as before.

What made things all the groovier was that just as she hit the apogee of her orbit my rocket blasted off. The pressures which had been building and building ever since the pygmy girl went to work on me with her washcloth suddenly cut loose. My muscles trembled and my head spun. A million shooting stars flashed in front of my eyes, and somewhere in the back of my brain a big brass band was playing "The Stars and Stripes Forever."

Like wow.

And double-wow.

And wow again.

As I disengaged myself from Vera's loving grip, I was trembling like a drunk with the DT's. I managed to stumble to the edge of the tub. Then I flopped down in a motionless heap.

Vera was even worse off than I was. She took two steps across the tub, then toppled over face first into the water. Two eunuchs promptly ran to her side and carted her away. Douzi squatted down alongside me and smiled satisfiedly.

"They don't often pass out like that, Damon," he said. "I'm proud of you, boy. Mighty proud."

"Thanks," I murmured.

Frankly I was proud of me too, but I was also becoming more than slightly apprehensive. If every day at the harem was like this day, I'd barely have the energy to walk, let alone to find the hidden bombs.

When Superman and his sexmate finished their round, we took another break. Then the pygmy girls with the washcloths went to work on us again. A few minutes later, I was going at it hot and heavy with the final cutie in my foursome, the tall blonde with the beautiful face.

In all honesty, I wasn't really in the mood for love; I was

84

in the mood for sleep. My manhood was holding up fine, but the rest of me was coming apart at the seams.

Still, I had my job to do, so I did it, and if the blonde was unhappy with the quality of my work, she sure as hell didn't show it. Her first orgasm was every bit the bell-ringer that her predecessor's had been, and while she didn't quite pass out after the second, she did require the assistance of a eunuch to make her way back to her seat.

The festivities now over, Douzi summoned the pygmies with the *nargilehs* and we all smoked some more hash. Then the tub was filled and everyone took a piping hot bath. This over, we adjourned to the *tepidarium* for a cool bath. Then the entire party moved to the vestibule, where we lounged around eating ice cold slices of melon and drinking steaming black coffee served up from a jewel-bedecked *finjan*.

The four girls whom I had entertained, along with a couple from Superman's group, crowded around me and made with some small-talk. I had a lot of questions to ask, but Douzi was never more than a few feet away, so I didn't dare ask them. Instead, I answered the girls' questions, most of which centered around my sex research projects. The dolls all seemed very interested, which was a good sign. Now, if only I could get them interested enough in me personally—and in my mission—that they'd tell me where the bombs were . . . if they knew!

Finally Douzi clapped his hands and the coterie of pygmies slipped out of the room. This was the signal that the time had come for our party to break up. One by one the girls paired off with their eunuchs and left. Then Superman and his eunuch left. Then Su Wing and her eunuch left.

What left Douzi and I and the last two eunuchs alone in the room. "Well," said my host, patting me on the small of the back, which was just about as high as he could reach without standing on tip-toe, "you've acquitted yourself admirably. From now on you may think of yourself as a permanent member of my household. Mazimba here"—he gestured toward the swishier of the two eunuchs—"will be your personal servant. He doesn't speak English well, but he understands enough of it to carry out routine orders. If you want anything, ask him and he'll get it for you."

Mazimba beamed happily. "I om ott your service," he said. His eyes darted to my groin, letting me know that there were absolutely no services excluded from his offer.

"As concerns your work schedule," Douzi went on, climbing into his uniform, "I think you'll find that the demands made on you are relatively light. Each evening at eight you will dine with the nine girls and Superman. On occasion Su Wing and I will join you, but more often than not we'll be elsewhere. After dinner there will be a social period of approximately an hour and a half. You, Superman and the girls will adjourn to the recreation room adjacent to the dining room, where you may chat, watch television, play chess or otherwise amuse yourselves.

"At eleven, you and Superman will go to your bedrooms. Shortly thereafter some of the girls will come to visit you. The order in which they appear will be determined by me or by someone whom I've appointed to take charge of the matter. Each girl will be entitled to an hour of your time, during which you'll be required to entertain her in any way she deems desirable. Occasionally, perhaps, all nine girls will visit you the same night. More often, however, you'll be visited by only four or five. The girl whose turn is last will be entitled to spend the rest of the night with you if she chooses. However, under no circumstances is any girl to remain in your room after nine a.m. At that time, all the girls are due in the dining room for breakfast. You may choose to have breakfast with them if you like, or you may abstain. In either case, the kitchen will always be open to you. Anytime you want something to eat, ask Mazimba and he'll get it for you.

"Festivities of the sort that took place this afternoon are not regular occurrences. They are held only on ceremonial occasions, or when my whims dictate it, which means once every week or two at most. Naturally you are required to participate each time a ceremony is staged, but the extra duty should not prove too burdensome. Besides, whenever a ceremony is staged, there's no sex duty that evening, so everything balances out.

"As to how you will pass the daytime, you may do

86

whatever pleases you. If you share Superman's tastes, you'll spend most of the time asleep or lounging around the outdoor pool. However, all facilities of the palace are at your disposal. You may use my library, my baths, my lake, my gardens or anything else which appeals to you. There are some areas on the grounds where you will not be permitted to enter, but these are carefully guarded, so there is no danger that you'll enter them accidentally.

"And that, my dear Damon, is what you can expect for as long as you stay here. If any problems arise which you would like to discuss with me personally, request an audience through Mazimba. As I said when we first met, every effort will be made to insure your comfort. All I ask in return is that you continue to satsify my female house guests as you did this afternoon." He rubbed his hands together, signifying that the speech was over. "Have you any questions?"

"Only one," I said weakly. "Where's my bed?"

He chuckled sympathetically. "Mazimba will take you there forthwith." He offered me his hand. "Now, sleep well, Damon. Tomorrow's another day, and judging from what I've seen this afternoon, you'll have a great many young ladies knocking on your door after dinner."

I bade Douzi goodbye, then followed Mazimba through a winding series of corridors to a large room overlooking the garden. The view was magnificent, and so were the furnishings of the room, but I was too bushed to pay attention to anything but the bed. It was big and soft and comfortable, and I flopped down on it without even bothering to undress. The last thing I heard was Mazimba's pledge that he would be at my beck and call if I needed him. He vanished into a small anteroom, and I closed my eyes. I went to sleep instantly.

CHAPTER SIX

When I woke up it was eleven the following morning. I had Mazimba fetch me a breakfast consisting of the Belgravian version of steak and eggs—elephant steak and duck's eggs, it turned out to be. Then my swishy eunuch and I took a walking tour of the palace and its grounds.

The palace was nothing less than sensational. Douzi had duplicated not only the *Hünkâr Hamami* of Muhammad II's digs in Constantinople but also the First Court, a two-story wing where Douzi's bureaucrats now attended to their paper-shuffling; the Second Court, or Court of the Divan, a three-story wing where the country's rubber-stamp National Assembly held its infrequent sessions; the Third Court, a four-story wing which housed the palace museum, library and treasury; the Fourth Court, a two-story wing where higher-ups among Douzi's lieutenants had their offices; and the various between-wing kiosks, which in Muhammad II's time had served as repositories for religious relics and which in Douzi's setup housed various secular art treasures.

The only areas to which I was denied admittance were the *selamlik*, or Douzi's personal living quarters; the *haremlik*, where the girls lived, and the treasury vault. Since the *selamlik* and *haremlik* were on the fourth floor of the main building, I wasn't too concerned that either might contain a secret passage to an underground hideaway where the bombs might be stored or the girls' laboratory might be located. But the treasury vault was a different matter. It was located on the ground floor of the Third Court, and could very well have doubled as a passage to some underground chamber. I resolved that I'd find out whatever I could about the vault—and do it as soon as I could.

The grounds were equally sensational. I had been impressed with them during my initial tour the day before. But then I had been too wrapped up in Su Wing's charms to notice many of their finer points. Now, doing a walk-through with Mazimba, I found that virtually every detail was a copy of the grounds surrounding *Topkapi Sarayi* in Constantinople.

I asked Mazimba to take me through the two complexes of smaller buildings located apart from the palace. He was all too pleased to conduct a guided tour of the nearer complex. It was called the Hall of the Eunuchs, and it served as quarters for, in addition to the eunuchs themselves, the palace's entire complement of service personnel and the members of the Palace Guard. But admission to the farther complex was strictly forbidden, and when I asked Mazimba what the complex contained, he replied that he didn't know.

I remembered that in Muhammad II's palace, the Hall of the Eunuchs was reserved for eunuchs only, and the other complex of buildings housed all the non-eunuch palace underlings. Evidently Douzi had crowded his entire staff into the Hall of the Eunuchs and was using the group of buildings in connection with his bomb project. Did these other buildings contain the girls' laboratory and/or the bomb storage place? If not, I'd be willing to bet they contained something else very closely tied in with the bomb.

My tour, all told, consumed four hours. When it was over I was hungry again, so I repaired with Mazimba to the dining room, where I lunched on some suspicious-looking African fish and some even-more-suspicious-looking African vegetables. Then I told my solicitious swish that I planned to spend the rest of the day ambling through the gardens on my own, and that he was free to do what he pleased. He replied respectfully that Douzi had told him to remain with me at all times. I grudgingly accepted his companionship, and set off a-walking again.

As I walked, I reviewed all the data I had accumulated since I arrived in Belgravia, and tried to piece together a workable plan of action. Falling back on techniques I'd been taught in the U.S. Army, I conducted my review by the numbers.

Number One: Lin Saong.

The Girl from CHILLER was unquestionably one of the most formidable foes I'd encountered in all my days as a Coxeman. What made things all the worse was that she wasn't supposed to be my foe. She was supposed to be my ally.

According to the original plan, I was supposed to inform her, via a miniature radio transmitter with which she had supplied me, the location of Douzi's bomb—if and when I found it. Meanwhile, a radioman from The Coxe Foundation was supposed to be monitoring my transmissions so that Walrus-moustache back in the States could keep abreast of developments and swing into action in the event that Red China tried the double-cross which everyone had more or less suspected it would try.

Now there was no question about the double-cross. Lin Saong had told me about it herself. But the radioman from The Coxe Foundation was dead, and I had no other line of communication with Walrus-moustache.

If I did locate the bomb before two weeks were up and if I did tell Lin Saong where it was, the Red China-backed Peoples' United Front would advance on Douzi's palace and try to dismantle the bomb. If the dismantling job was a success, it'd be a feather in the cap of Communism. And I, as the man who had made the whole thing possible, would be branded a traitor. If the dismantling job was a failure, I—and virtually every other man, woman and precocious child within eighteen skillion miles—would be a dead duck.

Meanwhile, if I failed to locate the bomb before two weeks were up, PUF would launch a full-scale attack against the Belgravian capital. The bomb then almost inevitably would explode, and when the mushroom cloud had settled, Communism would still have a feather in its cap. Indeed, comrades the world over would worshipfully hail the suicidally brave PUF forces for having stopped Douzi's nefarious bomb program before it became a threat

90

to everyone on earth, and Red China could bald-facedly claim that it never would have supported PUF had it known that the bomb would be exploded. I, of course, along with every other man, woman and precocious child within eighteen skillion miles, would still be a dead duck.

Number Two: Douzi's palace.

The place was a carbon copy of Muhammad II's *Tokapi Sarayi* in sixteenth century Constantinople. It had taken six years to build, and it couldn't have been constructed for less than twenty or thirty million dollars. Thanks to the nationalized duBeers diamond mines, Belgravia had more than enough money to do the job. But why had Douzi selected *Topkapi Sarayi* as his model and not, say, Buckingham Palace or the Kremlin. Was it just a matter of personal taste? Or was there more involved?

Number Three: Douzi himself.

No question about it, Belgravia's diminutive dictator was a riddle wrapped up in an enigma.

Case-in-point: He was the favorite son of Belgravia's dominant Guwai tribe, and had been educated in the best European schools. But if he had been groomed from childhood for a political career, how did it happen that his selected field of study was not economics or political science or some other discipline which would fit into plans of this sort but rather, of all things, psychiatry? Or if politics hadn't been his intended future when he went away to school, how did it happen that he returned to Belgravia in 1959 and very suddenly emerged as a principal force in his nation's drive for independence?

Second case-in-point: his ploy with the female physicists. According to the theory which Red China had advanced at the ultra-top-secret conference of nuclear powers at Geneva—and which theory the United States was inclined to accept—Douzi had lured the physicists to Belgravia to lecture at his National University, then had enticed them to stay and work on his nuclear program by offering them the sexual services of Superman.

Any way you looked at it, it was a brilliant caper—a caper certainly worthy of an Oxford- and Sorbonne-trained headshrinker. But if Douzi's main concern was getting the nine physicists to develop his bomb, how did it happen that he surrounded their sexual servicing with so many bizarre trappings, like the eunuchs and the pygmy men and girls—trappings which seemed to exist more for his own pleasure than for the pleasure of the physicists themselves?

Third case-in-point: his personal sexual tastes. Judging from what I'd seen so far, he was a walking composite case history from Krafft-Ebing's *Psychopathia Sexualis*. He delighted in humiliating eunuchs, he enjoyed homosexual acts, he was a leather fetishist, he was a voyeur *par excellence* and he also grooved on straight heterosexual congress. But he evidently had no desire for the physicists themselves. If he did, why did he fail to so much as touch one of them during the orgy in the *Hünkâr Hamami?* And he apparently was equally uninterested in the pretty pygmy girls who had participated in the ceremony. Why was he so interested in Su Wing?

The more I thought about him, the more questions I had—and the fewer answers.

Had the harem been set up chiefly for the femme physicists' benefit or chiefly for his own? If chiefly for their benefit, what use did he plan to put it to when they finished developing his bomb and ceased to be of use to him? If chiefly for his own, why wasn't he taking greater advantage of the libertine possibilities it offered?

Why had he let Su Wing become so intimately involved in the harem's activities? If he was intererested in her primarily for sexual reasons, wouldn't he have hidden her away somewhere where she'd be completely in the dark about the comings and goings of the femme physicists? If he had been intersted in her primarily as a double-agent, wouldn't he have pawned her off on one of his underlings in BELSO?

Why had he accepted virtually without question my wholly implausible story about my having defected to Red China and having been assigned to CHILLER on Su Wing's request? Hadn't he considered the possibility that I might have been a spy? And if so, why had he given me such free access to the femme physicists? Were my sexual talents so important to him? Couldn't he just as easily have augmented Superman's efforts with the efforts of another imported stud recruited via classified ads—or two imported studs, or four, or six, or nine?

Number Four: Su Wing.

Of everyone involved in the bomb business, she seemed to be the most on-the-level. But was she really as on-the-level as she seemed to be?

She had played sex games with me in the car under circumstances which might very easily had led to our being detected. And if we had been detected, CHILLER's goose would have been cooked along with mine.

If she was a dedicated Communist agent, would she have risked it? And if she wasn't a dedicated Communist agent, where did she stand? Had she perhaps double-crossed her Red bosses and assumed the role not of a pro-Commie triple-agent but rather that of a pro-Douzi quadruple agent?

How far could I trust her? Could I trust her at all?

Number Five: the femme physicists.

According to the theory which Red China had advanced and the other nuclear powers had accepted, Douzi's hold on them was mainly sexual. In view of the antisexualism of their Communist homelands, the theory made sense.

But the girls obviously knew that they would be useful to Douzi only until they developed his bomb. Did they think he would continue to support them, and to arrange for their sexual gratification, once the job had been done?

Furthermore, they couldn't fail to realize that having cast their lot with Douzi they'd never be able to return to their homelands again. Would all nine of them—not three, not six, but all nine—accept lifelong exile as the price of a few months, or a few years, or even a lifetime of sexual satisfaction?

Still on the subject of the femme physicists, how did it happen that Douzi rounded up a bevy of broads who were not only nuclear geniuses but also twenty-four-karat beauties? Wasn't it kind of odd that there wasn't a single loser in the bunch? If Douzi had been interested primarily in developing his bomb, would he have limited his recruitment to beautiful girls or would he have obtained the best brains he could get no matter what they looked like? On the other hand, if he had been interested primarily in beauty, how did he manage to assemble a group of brains so fantastic that in a few short months they were able to develop a weapon potentially more formidable than anything in the arsenal of any nuclear power in the world?

Questions, questions everywhere.

But how to answer them?

What to do?

This much was certain: I had to do something fast.

Unless I did before thirteen more days passed, the Peoples' United Front of Belgravia, supplied with Red Chinese airplanes and Red Chinese bombs, would blow Douzi's palace—and me—and, no doubt to their very great surprise, also themselves—right off the map. But where to start?

The logical place was with the nine femme physicists. Before the night was over, a few of them, and possibly more than just a few, would come knocking on my door for sexual servicing. It would be my job to give them the sexual show of shows, because unless I could win them away from Superman and get them to tell me where the bomb was hidden, I didn't stand a ghost of a chance of warding off the PUF attack on the palace.

But suppose they didn't know where the bomb was?

Or suppose they did know but couldn't safely tell me because my room was bugged?

And even if they did safely tell me, how could I get word to Lin Saong while Douzi's boy, Mazimba, was shadowing me every step of the way?

And even if I did get word to Lin Saong, how could I tip off Walrus-moustache about the double-cross?

And if I didn't tip off Walrus-moustache, how could I save my neck?

As a matter of fact, even if I did tip off Walrus-moustache, how could I save my neck?

Hadn't he said that once I had left for Belgravia The Coxe Foundation would officially refuse to recognize me?

Needed: one plan of action.

Amendment: needed very desperately, one plan of action.

Ha! Now to find one!

As I ambled around Douzi's palace grounds, I thought hard, but the harder I thought, the farther away I seemed from finding a solution to my dilemma.

Then suddenly an idea struck me.

It wasn't a solution, but with luck it might set me off in the right direction.

It came to me in a roundabout way.

As I strolled over the hills and through the dales of Douzi's grounds, my boy Mazimba complained that I was walking too fast for him. I slowed down, but soon he found it hard to keep up with me even when I was moving at a snail's pace. The three hundred-plus pounds he was carrying around with him were just too much baggage, and he was plumb tuckered out.

He had been told, of course, that he was to remain with me at all times. But if I set a more grueling pace than he could possibly maintain, he'd have no choice but to fall by the wayside. And if he fell by the wayside, I'd be able to break away from him long enough to take out my miniature transmitter and dash off a quick message to Lin Saong.

Not that I had anything to tell her at this stage of the game, but even though I had nothing to tell her, she couldn't very well stop me from transmitting. And if I transmitted long enough, there was just the slight possibility that my transmissions might eventually catch Walrus-moustache's ear.

This much I knew: When the dead radioman failed to report back to Washington in a day or two, my Coxeman-in-chief would wonder what was amiss.

And if sufficient time passed, he'd be curious enough to send someone to investigate.

Unless I missed my guess, the man who'd be sent to investigate would be another radioman, a man who could monitor the transmissions the dead man was supposed to have been monitoring.

And if I kept my wits about me I might just be able to

sneak something into those transmissions which would let my Coxeman friends know what was happening.

They had said they'd disown me if there were any slip-ups anywhere along the line.

But if I could manage to hip them to the double-cross that Lin Saong had in mind, they'd have no choice but to play the game my way, because I'd be the only guy who could pull the Free World's chestnuts out of the fire.

I was parlaying longshot on top of longshot on top of longshot, but it was the only bet on the board, and I had to gamble on it.

I started walking faster.

Mazimba begged me to stop and let him rest, but I just kept on walking.

He stumbled along after me, puffing like a steam engine.

Then, after about half a mile, he clutched his belly, dropped to one knee and toppled over on his side.

I knelt beside him. "Don't worry about a thing, buddy boy," I said cheerily. "Just go on back to my room and rest. I promise I won't tell your boss that you fell down on the job."

"But—but—" he protested.

"No buts about it. Either you go back to your room or I walk your legs off. Which'll it be?"

"No," he begged. "Please—"

"Yes," I grinned. "There's no other way."

He threw in the towel. "Okay. I go back. But please no tell boss. Please no tell."

I assumed him I wouldn't. Then, to make things easier for him, I walked back to the room with him.

He sighed with relief as I closed the door behind us. Then he staggered into the anteroom and flopped down on his bed. A few seconds later he was snoring like an old warhorse.

I rested for a few minutes myself. Then, taking Lin Saong's miniature transmitter from beneath the false bottom in my suitcase, I slipped outside.

The highest hill on Douzi's grounds was only a five-minute walk away. I hurried to the top and transmitted my first message. It was anything but short and to the point.

"Good evening, Lin Saong," I said in my best razzle-dazzle disc jockey's voice, "this is your old buddy, Rod Damon, broadcasting to you from high atop Melody Mountain in good old Belgravia. In a few minutes we'll have a word from our sponsor, but first here's a rendition by the Belgravian string quartet. Amendment: in a few minutes we'll have a word from the Belgravian string quartet, but first here's a rendition from our sponsor. Nope, that isn't right either, is it? Well, anyway, you get the message.

"And speaking of messages, have I got a few for you. Beep-beep, beepety-beep-beep-beep. Flash! President Albert Douzi, chief of state of the Republic of Belgravia, yesterday afternoon entertained nine girls at a king-size orgy in his palace. A good time was had by all. The star of the show was a newcomer to the palace, a sexologist by the name of Rod Damon, who stole the spotlight from stud-in-residence Fidel Superman by balling four chicks in the bathtub after balling one of their colleagues on a marble bench. All of which goes to show you, it sometimes pays to lie down on the job.

"Beep-beep, beepety-beep-beep-beep. Flash and double flash! The man who came to the palace looking for a certain hiding place didn't find it. But he found a few other things that interested him—and not all of them were between the legs of pretty girls. More about this development in our next broadcast, folks. Our team of on-the-spot newsmen is working diligently for further details.

"Beep-beep, beepety-beep-beep-beep. Flash! Yep, just a single flash this time, folks. Don't want to give you too much of a good thing, heh-heh-heh. As I was saying, flash! More news about that Damon fellow. In an interview this afternoon with certain reporters from this very station, he confessed that he really has the hots for a girl named Lin Saong. He revealed that while playing sex games with two of her subordinates, known only as Girl Number One and Girl Number Two, he noticed that Lin Saong's breasts were heaving passionately—this despite the fact that she claimed to be totally uninterested in such bourgeois capitalist pursuits as sex. According to Damon, the passionate heaving

97

of her breasts was evidence that she had the hots for him, which in turn gave him the hots for her. All of which leads us to believe that when the two of them get together again, there's going to be a hot time in the old town tonight.

"And that, folks, is today's newscast. But don't leave your trusty receivers, because who knows, we may have more news for you at any moment. Beep-beep, beepety-beep-beep-beep. Testing one, two, three, four, five, six, seven. Roger, wilco, over and out."

I tucked the transmitter back into its case, then slipped it into my pocket. Then I headed back to my room, pleased as all get-out that Lin Saong would soon receive a message that would leave her doing the slow burn to end all slow burns.

It wasn't just that I wanted to annoy her, although, after what she had put me through, the idea of annoying her wasn't exactly unappealing. But there was a more important method behind my madness. As a matter of fact, there were several important methods behind my madness.

For one thing, I wanted to get Lin Saong accustomed to receiving rather lengthy transmissions. I knew that Walrus-moustache's new radioman—if, in fact, there was one—wouldn't be in Belgravia yet. But when he arrived he wouldn't be able to find the beacon on which I was transmitting unless I really kept the airwaves burning. If I kept them burning now, when the new man could not possibly be around, Lin Saong would have no reason to become suspicious when I kept them burning later and he very well might be around.

For another thing, I wanted her to get used to receiving messages which were ninety-nine and forty-four one-hundreths per cent gibberish. Only if I did so would I have a chance of sneaking into the transmissions which might be intercepted by Walrus-moustache's man some information about the double-cross which Lin Saong and her Commie pals had in the works.

For still another, I wanted to persuade her that I was some kind of a nut. If she believed that I was a nut, she'd be likely to believe that the people I was working for were also a little screwy. And if she believed they were a little screwy, she might not expect them to do something eminently sensible—like sending a new radioman to replace the one whom she and her people had killed.

Of course, the practice of sending her long and whacky transmissions was not without its dangers.

First of all, there was always the possibility that Douzi's people might zero in on the beacon and trace the transmissions to me. But I was gambling on the hunch that had Douzi suspected me of anything he wouldn't have let me into his harem in the first place.

Secondly there was the possibility that Lin Saong might decide that I was too dangerous to have on her team and that I therefore should be eliminated. But the only way she could eliminate me would be to send someone into the palace to kill me. And Su Wing's alleged influence notwithstanding, I was pretty sure CHILLER wouldn't try go get a second agent into the palace so soon after I'd slipped in. Also, unless CHILLER had really needed me, they wouldn't have played ball with the United States in the first place. So, right now I was all they had going for them, and whether they liked me or not, they were struck with me.

Any way I sliced it my transmissions were risky, but I was better than halfway convinced that my approach to the problem was the safest approach there was. And safe or not, it was the only hope I had of getting out of the mess alive.

Back in my room, I slipped the transmitter back into the false bottom of my suitcase. Then, after checking out Mazimba to make sure he was still asleep, I combed the room for hidden microphones. Since all the evidence suggested that Douzi didn't suspect me of anything, I thought it unlikely that the room would be bugged. Still, that was where I'd be entertaining the femme physicists who wanted my services, and that was where I'd be trying to persuade them to tell me what they knew about Douzi's bomb. If he did suspect me, bugging my room would be the logical way to look for confirmation of his suspicions.

I searched everything from the mattress to the insides of

the hollow lampstands on the night table. I found nothing that suggested any bugging had been done.

Still not entirely sure that I was safe, but as sure as I could hope to be under the circumstances, I set my alarm clock for seven. Then I pulled shut the drapes, plunging the room into darkness, and went back to sleep.

CHAPTER SEVEN

I awoke to the feel of a cool, soft hand stroking my manhood.

Blinking the sleep from my eyes, I peered through the darkness. I had a sneaking suspicion that the hand belonged to my buddy Mazimba, and if I was right, he wasn't going to be my buddy anymore.

I was wrong. The hand belonged to a girl. I tried to make out her features, but I couldn't.

I glanced at the luminous dial of my wristwatch. It read six forty-five. Whoever my caller was, she was breaking Douzi's house rules.

"Vera?" I whispered, reasoning that if anybody would have a reason to sneak into my room, she would.

The girl's full, round breasts pressed against my arm, and her moist lips brushed my ear. "No, not Vera," she whispered back.

"Nadia?" I guessed.

"No, not Nadia."

"Olga?"

"Not Olga either."

"Then who? Su Wing?"

"No, not Su Wing."

I hoisted myself up on one elbow. "Then, who are you?"

Her face pressed gently against my shoulder. "You don't know me, but I want very much to know you. My name is Tania."

I reached across the bed and flicked on the night table lamp. In its dim light I saw a girl with short, raven black hair that fell around her ears in a coiffure reminiscent of Prince Valiant. Her eyes were a sexy ice blue. Her lips were

101

moist and hot pink. She was the doll who, at the previous afternoon's orgy, had been wearing a hopsack mini-robe that hung just an inch or two below the underslope of her buttocks, and who had been so hot to trot that she'd almost broken her eunuch's nose as it pressed into her most womanly places. She now was wearing a starched white lab coat, but she evidently was just as sexed-up as at the orgy. She continued to stroke my manhood with one hand, while with the other she guided my hand between two buttons of the lab coat and over the creamy soft curve of her belly.

"Nice to meet you," I said, meaning it sincerely. "But don't you think it's kind of risky coming to my room like this?"

A long, bare leg stretched out from beneath the lab coat, and a well-turned ankle rubbed provocatively against my calf.

"I was careful not to be seen coming here," she replied. "And I'll be just as careful leaving." An expression of concern crossed her pretty face. "But we haven't much time, so we mustn't get too involved in conversation." She began tearing open the buttons of the lab coat, revealing a sumptuous expanse of alabaster-white flesh covered only by the frilly fabric of her lacy red bra and bikini panties. "Quick, Damon," she said with sudden urgency, "make love to me."

I placed a restraining hand on her super-sexy hips. "I'd love to. But what about my eunuch? He's in the next room." As if on cue, Mazimba let loose with an elephantine snore.

She fought her way out of the lab coat, and with frantic fingers unhooked her bra. "He won't mind. The eunuchs here aren't at all possessive."

I felt desire flare up inside me as the bra fell away, exposing a pair of marvelously round, unbelievably white breasts. Their soft pink rosettes gave way to a pair of tantalizingly taut, proudly upthrust, blood-red nipples. "He might not mind," I allowed, my resistance rapidly waning. "But he could tell Dr. Douzi. Then you and I would both be in trouble."

She arched her hips and feverishly tugged her panties

102

over the sumptuous globes that were her buttocks. "He won't tell. The eunuchs hate Donzi as much as we girls do."

The panties inched over her thighs, and my eyes fixed appreciatively on the triangle of soft black hair covering her Mount of Venus. My desire soared, but the sudden revelation that both the girls and the eunuchs hated Douzi motivated me to curb my natural instincts. "Why do you hate him?" I asked.

The panties reached her knees. "Make love to me. When we're through I'll tell you all about it."

"Tell me all about it first. Then I'll make love to you."

Her legs moved in a quick bicycle motion, and the panties fell to her ankles. "Let's make love first."

"Let's talk first."

"No, let's make love first."

"Better yet, let's compromise." I cupped her breast, and my fingers moved teasingly over the tip of her eagerly distended nipples. "Tell me about it *while* we're making love."

She slipped one foot out of the panties. Then, with the other, she executed a neat little kick that sent them flying across the room. "It's a deal," she smiled. Whereupon she spread her legs wide and pulled me into place on top of her.

I entered her quickly. Her hips pressed hard against me, urging my manhood deep inside her. Then they began moving sideways in exciting counter-rhythm to my front-and-back thrusts. "Ah, Damon," she moaned, "that feels so good!"

It felt good for me too. In fact, it felt so good that I wanted nothing more than to prolong the feeling. But I remembered my mission. "We made a deal," I reminded her. "Start talking."

Her hip-tempo quickened. "In a moment, darling. Let's enjoy this for a while first."

I forced myself to stop thrusting. "Let's enjoy it while we're talking," I said sternly. "Now, why do you hate Douzi?"

She did a couple of quick bumps and grinds that evidently were designed to take my mind off the subject.

103

Then, when I remained motionless, she resumed her former pace. "We hate Douzi," she said, "because he's a tyrant. He claims that he wants only to keep us happy, but he makes us work eight and ten hours a day, seven days a week, and he constantly berates us for not being more efficient. He abuses the eunuchs horribly, and he abuses everyone else on his staff too. He keeps us locked up in this place like prisoners, and he—he—oh, Damon, do we have to talk about it now? What you're doing feels so good. Let me enjoy it."

I resumed thrusting. "Enjoy it, but keep talking. If you hate him so much, why do you continue to work for him? Why don't you just leave?"

She gasped at an especially deep thrust, and her sexy sideways movements became more agitated. "We don't leave because—ah, Damon, that's so good—because we don't dare to. If any one of us tried to get out of here, she'd be—oh, Damon, that's wonderful, so wonderful—she'd be killed. We don't dare leave. We don't—oh, that's beautiful. Damon, that's marvelous. Don't stop. Please don't stop . . ."

I stopped. "Do you realize what he plans to do with the bomb you're developing for him?"

"He—he—the bomb? What do you know about the bomb?" She stopped moving also.

"I know a great deal about it, but I want to know a great deal more. I want to know where he stores the bombs that have been built already. And I want to know how close you are to perfecting the bomb you're working on now."

For a moment she said nothing. Then, eyes wide, she asked softly, "Why do you want to know?"

I couldn't answer the question without tipping my hand, but judging from the way things had happened between us, she was about the least dangerous person in the place to tip my hand to.

"In addition to being a sex expert, I'm also a spy for the United Nations Security Council," I said, bending the truth a little. "The member nations of the Security Council have learned about Douzi's bomb tests, and I've been sent to investigate. One way or another, I'm ultimately going to

104

find out exactly what I want to know. When I do, I'll relay my findings to the Security Council, and appropriate action will be taken against Douzi's government. You can choose to cooperate with me—in which case I'll do everything in my power to see to it that you're not prosecuted for your role in the matter—or you can refuse to cooperate—in which case I'll do everything in my power to see to it that you're prosecuted and convicted." I paused for effect. Then, slowly resuming my hip movements, I said, "Are you with me or against me?"

Her ice blue eyes mirrored her consternation. "I—I don't know what to tell you," she stammered.

I lengthened my strokes. Almost involuntarily, her hips ground into action with me. "Just tell me where the bombs are stored and how close you are to perfecting the bomb you're working on now."

She began squirming passionately beneath me. "I—I don't know where the bombs are stored. And I don't know how close we are to perfecting the one we're working on now."

I thrust harder, making her squirm all the more fiercely. "I don't believe you."

Her legs coiled tightly around mine. Her fingernails dug into my back. "It's the truth. None of us girls know where the bombs are stored. And each one of us works on a different aspect of the new bomb's development, so we don't know how close it is to perfection." Her hips started flopping wildly. "But I'll tell you all about that later. I'm so close to—to—satisfaction. And it feels so good . . . so good."

I stopped moving again. "Tell me now."

Her whole body shuddered, and her feet beat at my buttocks as if trying to spur me back into action. "Oh, please start moving again! Please! Ever since I heard you were coming to Belgravia I've been dying to meet you. And after I saw you make love to the other girls, I couldn't wait to make love to you myself. *Please* start moving again! *Please!!!*"

My hips took up a slow, teasing rhythm. "Tell me now," I repeated.

105

"I will!" she gasped. "I will! But, oh, please, let's make love first. I—I—I wanted desperately to be one of the girls in your group at the orgy. I—oh, that feels good!—I— When Douzi assigned me to Superman's group instead of yours, I was heartbroken. And I worked harder today than I ever worked so I'd get a chance to be one of your first lovers tonight. But when Olga drew up the priority list, I was number eight. That's why I sneaked to your room early. I knew that if I didn't get to you now, I might have to wait until very late tomorrow morning. And I couldn't wait that long, Damon. It'd kill me. It'd—it *is* killing me! It's—it's—oh, Damon, let's talk later. Please let's talk later. This is so good, and I—I—"

I was by no means ready to halt our conversation. But I was willing to interrupt it temporarily. Her hunger for me was gratifying. And so were the rapidly accelerating sideways movements of her hips.

I began thrusting in earnest. Each stroke sent me far up inside her. She responded by taking up a spiral-like motion that sent shivers of sensation through me.

I thrust harder.

A fire of lust threatened to consume me. My manhood strained with excitement, and my pulse began pounding a mile a minute.

Tania was right up there on Cloud Nine with me. Her legs coiled around mine, and her hips ground feverishly. Her fingernails dug sharply into my back. Her mouth fixed to mine, and she hungrily sucked my tongue inside it.

We were on a nonstop express. Our bodies drew strength from each other, and each movement drove us closer and closer to the point of no return. My hands closed around her lush buttocks, pressing her against me. My manhood probed deeper and deeper.

Our timing was perfect. Just as I shot my fire into her, she abandoned herself to the sensations of her own orgasm. Her teeth dug ferociously into my neck. Her fingernails tore at the thick, hard flesh of my back. Her feet flailed wildly at my buttocks.

It lasted for all of a minute. Then her body went limp beneath me, and her eyes took on a glazed look. "Oh,

106

Damon," she sighed. "It was beautiful. Just beautiful."

I resumed thrusting in a slow, lazy rhythm. "Tell me more about Douzi," I said. "How did you happen to come to work for him?"

She hesitated for a moment, as if wondering whether she should tell me. Then her hips fell into tempo with mine, and she said, "It all started back when I was in Russia. I was working at the nuclear development laboratory in Kiev, and so was my husband. We didn't have much of a marriage. In fact, it was a marriage of convenience rather than love. But while divorce is accepted in Russia, it's frowned upon among high-ranking members of the scientific community. Consequently my husband and I remained nominally married, while actually we both sought our pleasures apart from our relationship—he with his first and greatest love, science, and I with a number of fellow scientists whom I believed to be discreet.

"Unfortunately one of these scientists was not nearly as discreet as I had taken him to be. He began bragging about his escapades with me, and word soon reached the ears of not only my husband but my boss, the chief of the nuclear development laboratory. A scandal seemed imminent—a scandal which would ruin both my career and that of my husband. The chief of the laboratory, seeking to avert such a scandal, suggested that I take a sabbatical leave.

"It was at precisely that time that I received through governmental channels an invitation to lecture for a semester at the National University of Belgravia. I wasn't especially eager to leave Russia, but the invitation gave me the perfect opportunity to get away from my husband and the impending scandal—at least for a while. At the urging of the chief of the laboratory, I accepted the invitation.

"When I arrived at the university, I was welcomed enthusiastically. I began my lecture series, and I conducted some private research at the university laboratory, the facilities of which were placed entirely at my disposal. About a month later I was invited to an informal dinner at the presidential palace. Superman was assigned as my escort. After the dinner he brought me back to my apartment and we made love. I don't have to tell you about his qualifications as a lover. And I don't have to tell you how pleased I was to have a man again after having remained abstinent ever since the potentially scandalous incident in Russia.

"A short while later I was again invited to the palace—this time for an interview with Dr. Douzi. After exchanging cordialities, he bluntly spelled out a proposition to me. He told me that he wanted me to move into his palace and begin working with some other nuclear physicists on a program his country was undertaking. He promised that I'd receive a generous salary and that I'd enjoy Superman's sexual services for as long as I worked on the program. I didn't know I'd been fed aphrodisiacs to make me constantly passionate.

"I didn't know at the time that the program involved development of a bomb. I was still suspicious, so I declined the offer. However, a few days later, Douzi summoned me for another interview. This time he had a new proposition, submitted in the form of a threat. He said that if I refused to work on his program he would complain officially to Russia that I had behaved shamefully while at the university. He added that criminal charges of 'indecent behavior' and 'lewd and lascivious conduct' would be lodged against me, and that I would be tried on these charges, convicted and sentenced to ten years in prison. I knew that Russia would not come to my defense, especially in view of the near-scandal at the nuclear development laboratory in Kiev. So, with many misgivings—but unable to see any other solution to the problem—I accepted the proposition."

I clucked sympathetically. "So that's how Douzi got you here—blackmail."

She nodded. "And that's how he recruited the other eight girls also. That and drugs. I've discussed the matter with each of them, and the circumstances in all eight cases were virtually identical. Each girl had been invited to Belgravia after having become involved in a sticky situation at home. Each had been treated to a night in bed with Superman. Then each had been coerced into coming

108

to work here in Douzi's laboratory."

"What happened after you started work?"

"When all nine girls had been assembled, Douzi appointed Olga as supervisor. Her job was to coordinate the research of all the others. Initially none of us knew that we were developing a bomb, but she evidently did, because it was she who assigned our various projects."

My eyebrows arched quizzically. "Are you talking about the same Olga I think you're talking about?"

"Yes. The one who was making love with you on the bench during Superman's performance yesterday after-noon."

I groaned. Talk about luck! The one girl who knew more about the project than anyone else couldn't tell me what she knew even if she wanted to because she couldn't speak English!

"I don't know how Douzi persuaded her to work on the project knowing that it involved a bomb," Tania went on. "But, of course, she had been lured to Belgravia just as the rest of us had, so it's safe to assume that blackmail was involved. In any case, the project began. Each morning at ten we girls report to the laboratory and received our assignments. Generally we work for eight to ten hours a day, sometimes longer. When work finally is over, Olga rates us numerically on what we accomplish for the day. The girl who has been rated number one is permitted to be Superman's first lover for the night, the girl who has been rated number two becomes his second lover, and so on."

"When did Olga get a crack at him herself?"

"She always took the number nine position. I don't know how Douzi persuaded her to accept such an arrangement, especially since Superman inevitably becomes surly after his first three or four girls. But, of course, the last girl on the list always got to spend the rest of the night with Superman, so maybe that was compensation enough for her."

"Is Superman a good lover?"

"Quantitatively, yes—at least in the beginning. Soon, however, he is mechanic. You know, no variety. Then he

109

becomes inattentive, and wants only to get the job done with as soon as possible. That's why Douzi brought you here. For the past month or so, the girls had been complaining that Superman wasn't satisfying them. The complaints became more bitter as time passed, and there was even talk about our deliberately slowing down the project. I'm sure that things never would have come to that point since all of us now know that Douzi is a man who will stop at nothing to achieve his goals. But apparently our sexual discontentment caused some concern, because here you are."

"Now that you know you're working on a bomb which could annihilate all mankind, why don't you stop working? Or why don't you at least make some attempt to throw the project off course? Is sexual satisfaction so important to you that you'll jeopardize countless human lives just to achieve it?"

"That's a hard question to answer. Actually, of course, we can't stop working. If we did, we'd all be killed—or we'd be subjected to tortures worse than death. And we can't throw the project off course, because Douzi has been following our work closely and would realize what was happening. Perhaps we should take a humanitarian view and say that our own lives are small enough a sacrifice to make when the world itself is in peril, but I'm afraid that none of us is quite that humanitarian. Besides, if one of us refused to work, there's no guarantee that the other eight would also refuse. And even if all nine of us refused, it's possible that Douzi could recruit other physicists to take up where we left off. Also—though this may be a rationalization—I don't think any of us believes Douzi will actually use the bomb. More likely than not, having developed it, he'll merely use the threat of it to intimidate other nations into doing his bidding. Isn't that what Russia and the United States both have done with their bombs?"

I could've debated the point, but an argument on international political ethics was the last thing I wanted at this stage of the game. "Where is your laboratory located?" I asked, abruptly changing the subject.

"On the palace grounds."

"In the cluster of heavily guarded buildings near the Hall of the Eunuchs?"

"Yes."

"And where are the fully developed bombs stored?"

"I don't know."

"Do you think Olga might know?"

"I doubt it. Douzi is very secretive, even with the people he trusts most. Generally the physicists who develop nuclear weapons for a nation are required to attend the tests of the weapons they've developed. But Douzi hasn't permitted any of us—not even Olga—to witness the tests of his bomb. We work in the laboratory until we've established a formula from which a bomb might be constructed. Then Olga turns over the formula to Douzi. Presumably the actual construction is entrusted to native Belgravian scientists."

"Might these scientists also be at work in the same buildings which house your laboratory?"

"No. The buildings are given over completely to us nine girls. I've been through every inch of them."

"How about the basements?"

"I've been through the basements too."

"Might there be a hidden passage leading from the basement to an underground worksite?"

"There might, but I really don't think Douzi would have the actual construction of the bombs done on the palace grounds. There's always the possibility that a bomb might detonate accidentally."

"Where would be the most logical place for the construction to take place?"

"As far away from population centers as possible—perhaps somewhere out in the Belgravian rain forests. The rain forests would be especially good sites because the climate is conducive to bomb storage. Also, the bombs could be shipped by river to the airport at Port duBeers in the event that Douzi ever decides to use them."

I was sure she was leveling with me, but I needed more information—information which she evidently didn't have. How to get it?

"Is there any other girl in your group," I asked, "who

might know more about this than you?"

"Only Olga, and as I said, Douzi doesn't tell her too much either."

"Will you try to find out from her anyway? Will you ask her and all the other girls in the group some discreet questions—questions that won't make them suspect you, but that might give me a lead I can follow up profitably?"

"I'll try," she promised.

I kissed her reassuringly on the nose. "Good. And don't let any grass grow under your feet. I have it on reliable authority that the Peoples' United Front plans to attack the palace in less than two weeks unless the United Nations intervenes. If the palace is attacked, and if any of the bombs are stored nearby, we're all liable to be blown to bits."

She gulped. "I'll really try, Damon. And I'll let you know what I find out the next time I see you."

"When will that be?"

"After dinner tonight. I'm only number eight on the list, but I'll wait my turn with you even if it means staying up all night. And I'll come to you every night from now on. Actually I planned to come to you anyway, because you excite me so. And now that I know how good you really are"—she gave my manhood a vigorous squeeze, as if to lend force to the compliment—"wild horses couldn't keep me away."

I responded to the flattery by giving her more to be happy about. She squirmed deliciously in reply to the increased vigor of my attack. "But don't sneak to my room anymore during forbidden hours," I warned. "We can't risk having anyone suspect us."

She nodded. "I won't. I—I—oh, Damon, it's starting to get very good again . . ."

The look in her eyes told me that I'd have to put the brakes on fast unless I wanted to lose her attention. But I didn't really have any more questions to ask her. And, frankly, my own attention was beginning to drift.

I picked up my pace.

She fell into tempo with me.

The feeling built and built and built until we both soared over the top together.

When it was over, she dressed and slipped out of the room. Then I showered, shaved and woke up Mazimba. It was time for dinner.

I entered the dining room feeling more confident than I'd felt since I fell into Lin Saong's clutches back at Port duBeers. I was safely inside Douzi's harem, I had come up with a plan to tip Walrus-moustache off about Red China's double-cross and I'd even managed to enlist the services of a femme physicist as a spy. Now, if my luck stayed good, things'd really get hopping in no time flat.

CHAPTER EIGHT

Things got hopping all right.

But my luck didn't stay good.

For a while it was fair.

Then it very rapidly turned bad.

Then it got worse.

And by the time the week was up, I felt like the guy they invented the word "jinx" for.

Dinner went swimmingly, as did the social hour which followed, as did the subsequent bedroom action. All told, seven of the nine femme physicists stopped by my room for sexual servicing, including Tania and Olga, the latter of whom wound up spending the night. But Olga couldn't speak English, and Tania hadn't been able to find out anything she hadn't already told me. Meanwhile, not wanting to tip my hand to too many people, I had refrained from questioning the other five girls too intensively; my innocuous queries got innocuous answers, and when Olga finally left at nine in the morning, I was no closer to solving the mystery of Douzi's bombs than I had been when Tania left my room just before dinner.

The night's carnal carnival had left me so pooped out that I didn't even bother to eat breakfast. Instead, I racked out until two in the afternoon. Then, after lunching on some rare Belgravian delicacy that looked like mud and tasted like what Army cooks euphemistically call "S.O.S." (real name: creamed chipped beef on toast), I went about the business of walking the legs off my boy Mazimba so that I could get away from him long enough to beam another transmission at Lin Saong.

The eager-to-please eunuch must really have eaten his

Wheaties, because it took me all of four hours to get him weary enough to call it quits. Finally, just before seven, he packed it in and headed back to my room. That left me with little more than an hour to make my broadcast, shower, shave and dress for dinner.

Hurrying to the hill from which my previous transmission had been beamed, I uncased the transistorized contraption which Lin Saong had given me. Then, putting on my razzle-dazzle disc jockey's voice, I began.

"Hellooooooo out there in spy-land. This is your old record-spinnin' buddy, Rod Damon, with another program of platters and chatter from high atop Melody Mountain in good old Belgravia. There won't be too many platters today, because there's lots and lots of chatter—and I really think you ought to listen close, 'cause the chatter's gonna be right up your alley. But first, for the benefit of all you music lovers out there, you hand-holding teenyboppers, and you blissfully wed young marrieds, and you middle aged grandpas and grandmas who still have what it takes, and even you lonely old men with walrus-like moustaches—yes, for all of you, from all of me, here's a song—that's 'song,' as in Lin Saong—the spelling's different, but the name's the same, and the girl who owns the name—are you listening, you old men with the Walrus-like moustaches?—yes, the girl who owns the name is a real beauty, a real knockout, the type of chick you just gotta flip for, even if—and that's a cue, orchestra leader, if I ever heard one—"

I hummed a four-bar intro, then went into a nasal rendition of an old hillbilly tune titled *She Done Me Wrong*. The tune didn't really contain any clues about her double-crossing me, but just the title of it should be enough to give Walrus-moustache the gist of what had happened—if he was listening in. Meanwhile, the two minutes-plus that it took me to warble my way through the three verses and four choruses might help whoever was trying to intercept my beacon to zero in on me loud and clear.

The tune over, I resumed chattering. "And now for the news. Item A from Melody Mountain today deals with a cluster of buildings. There are three clusters of buildings on the neatly manicured grounds of Dr. Albert Douzi's estate here in Belgravia. The first of these is the mammoth presidential palace. The second is the Hall of the Eunuchs, where Dr. Douzi's housekeeping crew passes its off-duty hours. The third is an unnamed cluster that is very heavily guarded. Those of you out in radio-land who may have wondered about certain scientific goings-on here at the estate probably suspected that this third and unnamed cluster of buildings serves as the laboratory where Dr. Douzi's task force of female physicists is working feverishly to develop a bomb. Well, I can now confirm your suspicions. The physicists are indeed working here to develop the bomb. And they're working hard. But they're not making as much progress as Dr. Douzi would like. In fact, according to authoritative sources who have spoken personally to this reporter, the bomb program has fallen far behind schedule. So, if any of you have been worried that the bomb would be ready in two weeks—or any similarly brief time interval—forget it. You've got nothing to worry about. Call off your attacks, kiddies. You'll only be wasting your time if you don't."

Abandoning the disc jockey patter-pattern for a moment, I continued, "And listen closely, Lin Saong. I haven't yet discovered the exact location of the bombs which Dr. Douzi now has in storage, but I can say without qualification that the bombs are not—I repeat, are not—stored anywhere on the palace grounds. The storage spot is somewhere in the Belgravian interior. In a few days I'll be able to tell you exactly where. Meanwhile, just stay cool, and above all, don't do anything rash like sending the boys from PUF to attack the palace. If you do, you'll destroy the only chance you have of getting to the bottom of the mystery."

Still addressing Lin Saong, but speaking mainly for the benefit of Walrus-moustache, I added, "I realize you might think I'm feeding you false information, sweetie. And you have every reason to think so. After all, if PUF attacks the palace in two weeks, as you told me it would when you announced that Red China was double-crossing the United States, I'd be killed along with everyone else, and of course

116

dead counterspies can tell no tales. But hear me out, baby. I'm not being vindictive. I'm not trying to get revenge on you for reneging on your deal and for killing the radioman who accompanied me to Belgravia. I'm just trying to get out of this mess alive. And I know that the only way I can get out alive is by playing ball with you. I'm playing ball, honey. I'm playing ball like I never played ball before. Trust me—just like the United States trusted you. You'll find that I, like the United States, can be counted on to keep my word—even though you and your creepy Commie comrades can't."

It was a pretty blatant spiel, I realized. And I was more than mildly suspicious that Lin Saong would understand exactly what I was trying to accomplish with it. But things were moving too fast for me to bank on a more subtle pitch. And anyway, whether Lin Saong could see through my stratagem or not, there wasn't too much she could do to stop me. I was on the inside of Douzi's harem, looking out; she very definitely was on the outside, looking in.

Content that I wasn't taking any more chances than I had to, I did another hillbilly tune for the benefit of the radio interception squadron which Walrus-moustache hopefully would already have dispatched to Belgravia. Then I repeated my spiel about why PUF shouldn't attack Douzi's palace, signed off and headed back to my room. Dinner, and the subsequent round of sexual shenanigans, were only forty-five minutes away.

As on the previous evening, dinner went like a charm, as did the social period, as did the bedroom action. This time six of the nine femme physicists visited me for sexual servicing, again including Tania and Olga, the latter of whom again wound up spending the night.

Still playing my cards close to my vest, I refrained from asking the four other girls any questions which would give away my identity as a spy. But Tania brought me an interesting item of information.

During the day, it seemed, she had been taken off the project she was working on and assigned to another one, this time as Vera's collaborator. The implication was that some breakthrough had been made in the development program, a breakthrough which rendered Tania's previous line of research unnecessary. Evidently the perfection of the super-bomb was now a lot closer to being realized.

Tania left me at five o'clock that morning and Olga took her place. Because of the language barrier, I couldn't probe for information about the project at the laboratory. But I did do my usual bang-up sexual job. Olga and I frolicked right up to the last minute of the nine o'clock curfew, and when she left I was sure of one thing. If I ever did figure a way to break the language barrier, here was one girl who'd have plenty of motivation to tell me what I wanted to know.

But how to break the barrier?

I had no idea.

Meanwhile, time was passing quickly.

And as I thought about the passage of time, I realized that luck really had turned against me.

The way things were set up, the only hours I could really call my own were those between the time I woke up and the eight o'clock dinner hour.

To do anything during those hours that would be beneficial to my mission, I had to shake my ever-present tail, Mazimba.

And if I couldn't figure out some way to shake him other than walking him into exhaustion, I'd barely have time enough to make my daily broadcast to Lin Saong, let alone to explore any of the other avenues of inquiry that might lead to a solution to the problem.

Worse yet, now that I thought about it, there really weren't too many avenues of inquiry to explore.

There was, of course, the matter of the treasury vault, admission to which had been denied me. Ever since I'd learned of the vault, I'd wanted to try to get a look inside. But even if I did manage to shake loose a few hours to make an attempt at checking the vault, how would I get past Douzi's guards?

Another possibility was Superman. As the palace's longtime stud-in-residence, he might very well have heard something from one or another of the femme physicists which would be valuable to me. But judging from what I'd seen so far, Superman liked me like little boys like castor oil. Could I afford the time I'd need to get on his good side, when the only result of warming up to him might be the discovery that he really hadn't heard—or hadn't paid attention to—any of the girl's comments which might shed light on the bomb development program?

Then there was the cluster of buildings which served as the girls' laboratory. If I could get inside, I might see something which to Tania might not necessarily have seemed worth mentioning but which to me might be very significant. But how could I get inside?

Yes, any way I sliced it, my avenues of inquiry were limited, and there was no guarantee that if I looked down one or more of them I'd find anything even remotely helpful to me.

What to do?

The only thing to do, it appeared, was to keep plugging as I had been plugging—to continue beaming my chatter-riddled transmissions to Lin Saong in the hope that one of Walrus-moustache's boys would intercept them, and to continue working hand-in-hand with Tania in the hope that she might come up with some useful information.

But both of these were slim hopes, and the more I thought about it, the slimmer they seemed to be.

Slim-hope-number-one: the radio transmissions.

All told, only four days had passed since the night back in Port duBeers when Lin Saong informed me that the radioman who had accompanied me to Belgravia was dead. If the radioman had had instructions to report back to Walrus-moustache as soon as he had arrived in Belgravia and to give progress reports at regular intervals thereafter, the death might have been discovered almost immediately and a new man might have been dispatched in short order. Then, if the new man had managed to get set up without running afoul of CHILLER, it was possible—remotely possible—that he'd now be tuned in on my transmissions to Lin Saong and that he'd be relaying what I said back to Walrus-moustache in the States.

But suppose that the first radioman hadn't been told to keep in constant touch with Walrus-moustache. Suppose

119

instead that for security reasons—or for whatever reasons spy-types like Walrus-moustache might have—he'd been told not to report in until he had come up with something very concrete. In that case, Walrus-moustache still would not know that the man was dead, and my info-laden transmissions would be a total waste of effort.

Slim-hope-number-two: Tania's leads.

No question about it, the ravishing Russian with the ice blue eyes and the maddeningly beautiful legs had told me a lot. And from where I sat, it looked like she was going to tell me a lot more—as soon as she found out what I wanted to know.

But would she ever find out?

And if she did, would she find out soon enough for her findings to be useful to me?

If a breakthrough had been made in the development program, it might be just a matter of days before Douzi's bomb was perfected. Meanwhile, Tania's only sources of information were the other femme physicists, who more than likely didn't know anything more than she did.

The exception to the rule was Olga, who might know a great deal more, but according to Tania, Olga was stand-offish and very secretive. How could she be persuaded to loosen up?

Then, too, I had to consider the possibility that Tania wasn't leveling with me. Maybe she had gone to Douzi or to one of Douzi's henchmen after our initial confrontation and reported that I was a spy. If so, she might have been told to play along with me, feeding me false or useless information to lull me into a false sense of progress while the bomb development program speeded away in other directions.

Could I trust her?

And if I couldn't, who could I trust?

As I lay exhausted on my bed after my second night of servicing the babes in the Belgravian harem, I wondered.

And the more I wondered the more confusing the whole situation became.

After my welcome-aboard orgy at Douzi's *Hünkâr Hamami*, I had pondered a number of questions—

120

questions which made this caper one of the wackiest mysteries I'd ever tackled.

Now I pondered the questions again.

Question: If Douzi's main reason for attending to the sexual wants of his nine femme physicists was to keep them happy while they were developing his bomb, how did it happen that he surrounded their sexual servicing with so many bizarre trappings like the eunuchs and the pygmy girls, trappings like the elaborate reconstruction of Muhammad II's palace, trappings which seemed to exist more for Douzi's own pleasure than for the pleasure of the girls themselves?

Question: If Douzi had been groomed from childhood for a political career, how did it happen that his selected field of study was psychiatry rather than one of the social sciences which would be of value to him as a head of state? Or, if politics hadn't been his intended future when he went away to school, how did it happen that he returned to Belgravia in 1959 and very suddenly emerged as a principal force in the nation's drive for independence?

Question: Why had he let Su Wing, whom he knew to be a Red Chinese agent, become so intimately involved in the harem's activities—so involved, in fact, that it was upon her recommendation that he brought me into the harem . . . me, whom he would have every reason to suspect of being a spy? According to her, he believed that he and his goons had coerced her into becoming a double-agent, but was he gullible enough to accept her pledge of fidelity to his cause without even considering the possiblitity that she might really be a triple agent, still very much on the payroll of the Red Chinese?

Questions, questions everywhere.

But how to answer them?

I let my imagination run loose, and a hypothesis slowly took form.

At first it seemed ridiculous, but the more I thought about it, the less ridiculous it seemed.

All along I had operated on the unquestioned assumption that Douzi was in fact working to develop a bomb. And it was because of this assumption that so many of his

121

actions and attitudes had seemed inconsistent.

But the assumption was based exclusively on a theory advanced by the Red Chinese, who, if my hypothesis was valid, whould have every reason in the world for advancing a phony theory.

I now put aside the assumption and tried to visualize the situation at the Belgravian palace as I might have visualized it had I replied to Douzi's classified ad for a superstud without ever suspecting that a bomb was being developed on the premises. The picture that took form wasn't nearly as hard to accept, and it permitted me to make a few very interesting guesses about the role of Red China in the whole affair.

Had I replied to Douzi's classified ad without suspecting that he was trying to develop a nuclear bomb, my first impression would have been that the pint-sized president of Belgravia was a certified sex nut. And thinking of him as a sex nut rather than as a politician who sought to disrupt the world balance of power, I could very easily understand why he had done much of what he had done.

He was the favorite son of Belgravia's dominant Guwai tribe. Consequently he had been packed off to Europe so that he could be educated in the best schools. If my hypothesis was correct, he had been sent not with the hope that he would one day return to lead his country's drive for independence, but only with the hope that he would make a good life for himself—a life which his tribesmen in Belgravia might themselves never enjoy but a life the enjoyment of which they fervently wished for him.

So he went to Europe, and he became interested in psychiatry. Why psychiatry? Maybe just because it appealed to him. More likely, for the same reason that many other people become interested in psychiatry—because they think there's something wrong with them and they want to find out what.

What was wrong with Douzi? His problem was primarily sexual. He dug homosexual acts and leather fetishism as well as conventional heterosexual relations. He wanted to rid himself of these socially taboo tastes, and he thought psychiatry would help him do so. It didn't—but it did teach

122

him to live with them, and to take sexual satisfaction in whatever way he could and wherever he could find it.

But another problem arose; namely, where to find it? Douzi was a Negro, a pygmy and the possessor of underdeveloped genitalia. It's hard enough for a sexual deviate to find desirable partners if he happens to be white, normal-sized and abundantly endowed phallically. If he has going against him everything that Douzi had going against him, forget it.

But Douzi didn't forget it. After bouncing around Europe for a while, he returned in 1959 to Belgravia and found the political climate there considerably different from what it had been when he had left. Indeed, there was a movement underway for national independence, and he, as a favorite son newly returned with a prestigious European education, became a leader in the movement. When independence was granted, he drew up a constitution calling for an autocratic government in which he held the reins of power. Then, shortly after he took office, he went to work reconstructing the sixteenth century pleasure palace of Muhammed II where he, the sexually frustrated President Douzi, could cavort to his heart's content.

How the femme physicists entered the picture remained a mystery. Maybe Douzi lured them to Belgravia to put them to work on a nuclear project that didn't involve a bomb. Perhaps he wanted an atomic power plant or some other facility which harnessed nuclear energy for peacetime purposes. Whatever the case, he hadn't set up the elaborate sexual enterprises of the palace for their benefit; he had set them up for his own benefit.

Then, somewhere along the line, the Red Chinese learned about his setup and decided to capitalize on it. They exploded a couple of bombs in the South Atlantic—bombs which weren't as sophisticated as some which Red China previously had exploded, and which therefore might seem to be the handiwork of a newcomer to the ranks of the world's nuclear powers. The United States, Russia and the rest of the nuclear powers accepted Red China's theory that these bombs had been exploded by Belgravia, and I was sent to investigate.

123

Now, I was investigating, but the bombs I was looking for actually didn't exist. The whole investigation was a farce, set up by Red China to con the other nuclear powers. I'd be permitted to prowl around Douzi's palace for a while, reporting to Lin Saong at every step of the way. But Lin Saong would be the only person to receive my reports, and the United States and the other nuclear powers would never learn that what I had discovered was actually nothing.

Then, when I'd been on the scene long enough to give the Red Chinese con game an air of legitimacy, troops from PUF would attack the palace—perhaps detonating a small atomic device which had been planted there especially for that purpose. Red China could then claim that it had backed the PUF attack because I, a representative of the joint nuclear powers, had disclosed that Belgravia indeed had developed a bomb. The United States might deny that I was working on the case. But Red China would still come out of the whole affair smelling like a rose. More likely than not, they would say that they had been assured that the bombs were not stored on the palace grounds, and that they had therefore backed the PUF attack hoping that the bombs could be discovered after the reins of Belgravia's government had been wrested from Douzi's fiendish hands.

If this was the plan, it would explain why Su Wing enjoyed such freedom at Douzi's palace and why she had been able to work me into the harem without his raising an eyebrow. Douzi, far too wrapped up in his sexual hijinks to give any serious consideration to the business of espionage, never dreamed that either she or I would be dangerous to his nation's security. And he wasn't afraid that either of us would uncover the secret of his bomb, because he didn't have any bomb that we could uncover the secret of!

Of course, my little theory wasn't exactly flawless.

For one thing, I already had Tania's word that she and the other femme physicists knew they were working on a bomb. For another, if the only reason Lin Saong had sent me to the palace was to be a pigeon, she hardly would have been likely to give me a radio, the transmissions from which might be intercepted by anyone from the dead radioman's replacement to Douzi's own counterintelligence squad in BELSO. For a third, Douzi had been very emphatic in his instructions that I shouldn't inquire too closely into the femme physicists' activities or their reasons for being at the palace; if he had nothing to hide, he had nothing to fear.

But maybe Tania wasn't leveling with me after all. Maybe she'd been roped in by Lin Saong just as I had. After all, it was Tania who had come to me, not I who had come to her. And while she didn't say anything about the bomb until I brought the subject up, if she had been in cahoots with Lin Saong she'd have known well in advance that I would bring it up.

Also, Lin Saong might have given me the radio because she never dreamed that Walrus-moustache would send another man to replace the one who had been killed. It would have been a serious mistake on her part, but everyone makes mistakes now and then. Or maybe she *wanted* my transmissions to be intercepted. Their interception would lend credence to Red China's claim that Belgravia was developing a bomb. And if the United States later officially denied that I was in Belgravia on a spy mission, Red China could contest the denial, especially if Lin Saong had been recording my messages. Indeed, tapes of my messages would be invaluable to the Red Chinese; the tapes could be edited and altered to say whatever Red China wanted me to say.

As concerned Douzi's instructions that I shouldn't be too curious about the femme physicists' activities or their reasons for being at the palace, maybe he *did* have something to hide—not the development of the bomb perhaps, but something else, something which right now I could only guess at. For that matter, maybe the only thing he wanted to hide was the manner in which he had lured the girls away from their homelands.

Yes, the theory might have had its flaws, but the flaws could be explained.

And if the explanations weren't perfectly satisfactory, the fact remained that the no-bomb theory was still a hell of a lot more feasible than any yes-bomb theory I could think of.

Or *was* it more feasible?

The more I thought about it, the less convinced I became.

And the less convinced I became, the more I realized how much I needed additional clues—clues that would help me piece together some of the missing parts in this crazy puzzle that seemed to be getting crazier all the time.

But where to get the clues?

Superman?

The treasury vault?

The seven femme physicists—Olga and Tania excluded—whom I hadn't yet questioned?

Douzi himself? Did I dare risk telling him point-blank what Red China had up its sleeve, then let the chips fall where they may?

I recalled the old adage: any port in a storm.

I amended it to: every port in a storm.

Well, not quite every port.

I wouldn't open up with Douzi. At least not yet.

But I'd sure as hell chase down all the other possibilities. The time had come to stop playing my cards so close to my vest. I needed action, and I needed it fast.

The seven femme physicists wouldn't be hard to get to. I could count on at least three or four of them visiting me after dinner, and I was pretty sure that the others would make the scene at least once during the next couple of days. Caution be damned, I was going to lay my cards on the table with every last one of them, just as I had with Tania.

I'd also tackle Superman. Maybe my abundantly endowed competitor would be completely in the dark about what was happening. Or maybe he wouldn't tell me what he knew. But I owed it to myself—and to my mission—to find out whatever I could from him.

Also, I'd try to get into the treasury vault. It wouldn't be easy, but then, nothing in this whole deal was easy. To quote my buddies in the old United States Army Air Force,

"The difficult we do immediately; the impossible will take a little longer."

Finally, I'd grill Olga. There was a language barrier, to be sure. But as I lay in the bed which she left, supremely satisfied, just a short while before, I suddenly realized a sure-fire way to bridge that barrier.

Yes, I told myself, I really was going to swing into action. Time was wasting and I couldn't afford to waste another minute of it.

I looked at my watch.

It was nine forty-five.

I was exhausted after my night of nonstop sexual hijinks, and I wanted nothing more than to sleep.

But my ever-present Mazimba was racked out on his bunk, and I saw the opportunity to get in a few uninterrupted hours of work.

Dragging myself out of bed, I tugged on a pair of slacks and a sportshirt. Then I took Lin Saong's miniature transmitter from the false bottom of my suitcase, and hightailed it to the top of the hill I had dubbed Melody Mountain.

My broadcast was virtually identical to the one I had beamed out the previous afternoon—except that I sang eight hillbilly songs instead of two and repeated my spiel about why PUF shouldn't attack Douzi's palace five times instead of once. All told, I was on the air for more than an hour. If Walrus-moustache's radioman was in Belgravia, he had ample opportunity to zero in on my beacon. And if he zeroed in he had a damned good idea of what I was facing.

The broadcast over, I hurried to the Third Court of the palace and mingled with the bureaucrats in the offices of the Belgravia treasury. I knew I'd need a lulu of a story to con them into letting me into the vault, and I couldn't think of one. But while I was trying, I spotted a pile of bulky sacks being unloaded from an armored truck parked outside the back door.

The guys who were unloading the sacks were black-skinned natives wearing khaki uniforms and pith helmets.

127

There were four of them, and they carried their cargo through a bustling office area and into the vault, which was wide open. No one seemed to be paying any attention to them except an armed guard, who was leaning lazily against the truck.

I got an idea. It was risky in the extreme. But this was my day to take chances.

Slipping around to the rear of the building, I tiptoed through a narrow alley and into the courtyard where the truck was parked. The courtyard was deserted, and the position of the truck was such that the guard leaning against it couldn't be seen from any of the windows in the bordering buildings. I moved silently into place behind him.

He was just about my size, and he was toying with his billy club. The pistol in his holster glistened brightly in the morning sun. Glancing around to make sure I was unobserved, I moved closer to him. I waited until the sack carrier at the rear of the truck had vanished into the treasury building. Then, with one quick motion, I whipped the pistol from its holster and jabbed it into the guard's back.

"Don't say a word," I hissed. "Just keep your hands where they are and back up toward me."

He didn't budge. I wasn't sure whether he was dumbstruck by the suddenness of my move or whether he just couldn't speak English.

I took a step backward. "Come on," I growled. "Back up."

He said something in a Belgravian tribal tongue. I didn't comprehend a word of it, but nonetheless I had a pretty good idea of what he was trying to say: he *didn't* speak English.

I smiled. One thing was certain. He was a pro, and pros never play hero.

He might not have understood my instructions, but he knew that I meant business.

His billy dangled impotently from its strap, which hung loosely from his outstretched fingers. His other hand inched into hammer lock position behind his back, the fingers open. In his own professional way, he was letting

128

me know that he planned to be a cooperative prisoner—cooperative even to the point of not doing anything which would look suspicious to passersby, like raising his hands over his head.

I confiscated his billy, then took hold of his arm and slowly turned him around. His sweat-beaded black face wore an expression of just-mild concern. His small brown eyes fixed to mine, seemingly pleading with me to be the same kind of no-heroics pro that he was being.

I gestured with the gun toward the cab of the truck.

He dutifully climbed inside.

I pantomimed undressing.

He promptly stripped to his shorts.

I motioned for him to turn around.

He did.

I used his belt to tie his arms behind his back. Then I used my handkerchief to gag him. This accomplished, I took off my clothes and put on his uniform. Then, tugging the pith helmet over my eyes, I picked up a sack from the rear of the truck and carried it into the building.

I don't know how I got to the vault without anyone noticing my Caucasian face or the Caucasian arms that were sticking out of the short sleeves of his khaki shirt. But nobody stopped me. I entered the vault, put down my sack and began looking around.

What I found was exactly what you might expect to find in a vault—money, banknotes, stock certificates and a whole mess of official-looking papers.

But I didn't find anything even remotely resembling a bomb. And a detailed inspection of the vault's walls and floors failed to produce any evidence of a trapdoor or panel which might lead to a secret underground passage.

I couldn't figure out why Douzi had declared the vault off-limits to me. But it was painfully apparent that I had taken one hell of a crazy risk—and all for nothing.

I slipped out of the vault and headed back to the truck. This time I didn't even have a sack to shield me from the observation of the bureaucrats who were working there. But still none of them noticed me.

I wondered if maybe my luck, which had been just fair

for nearly three days now, was suddenly going to take a turn for the better.

For a while it seemed like it was.

At the truck, I changed back into my own clothes, tucked the guard's pistol inside my slacks, tossed his uniform across the front seat, and took off for Melody Mountain—all without being seen by anyone.

Then I beamed another hour-long transmission at Lin Saong—again without creating any noticeable stir.

Then, as I ambled back to my room, the bad luck started.

CHAPTER NINE

Mazimba wasn't waiting there for me. Another eunuch was.

"I have been sent to replace Mazimba," he said in labored English. "My name is Lumombe. I will do your bidding, and I will stay with you at all times."

I groaned. Bad Break Number One: I evidently had outsmarted myself by giving Mazimba the slip once too many times. Now I had a new tail, and this one was in a lot better physical condition than his predecessor. I might walk my legs off before I got him weary enough to fall out. Worse still, if Douzi questioned Mazimba, the pint-sized president might suddenly get the idea that I wasn't quite so harmless as I at first might have seemed.

After Lumombe and I had taken a lunch break, I hunted down Superman. I finally found him at the outdoor pool, basking in the sun while he glanced through an American girlie magazine full of nude and seminude photos.

I exchanged a few banalities with him, speaking very rapidly so that I could test Lumombe's English comprehension. It took less than a minute for me to realize that my new castrated companion didn't have the vaguest idea of what I was saying.

I sighed with relief. It seemed as though my luck was turning good again.

Ha! Bad Break Number Two!

Lumombe might not have understood me when I started pumping Superman for details about the nine femme physicists and about Douzi's comings and goings. But while Superman understood me perfectly, he refused to believe that I was trying to foil a plot involving Red China.

131

"I'm on to your game, Damon," he snarled. "You want to get something on me so you can have all the chicks in the harem for yourself."

"Don't be an idiot," I told him. "I can't even handle the chicks I have now."

"Well, I can. So if you get tired, just pack up and go home. Meanwhile, stop bugging me."

And that was that. I'd been operating on the theory of every-port-in-a-storm. But all the damned ports were closed—at least to my ship.

I did a quick walking tour of the palace grounds with Lumombe, hoping against hope that, appearances to the contrary, he'd prove to be as out-of-shape as Mazimba. I might just as well have tried growing wings. He finished the tour looking like he was ready to run the mile in less than four minutes. Meanwhile, my butt was dragging so low that I was sure it'd scrape the ground any second.

I thought of trying to bribe Lumombe to leave me alone. But I was pretty sure that Mazimba had taken a few lumps for dereliction of duty, and the odds were good that Lumombe would be afraid to accept a bribe. Worse yet, even if all the eunuchs hated Douzi, as Tania had said, fear might impel Lumombe to report the bribe offer, in which event I'd really be in hot water.

Nope, bribery was out of the question. And so, it seemed, was every other stratagem I had in mind.

Resigned to having him tag along after me, I abandoned my plan to beam another hour-long radio transmission at Lin Saong, and instead returned to my room. It was four fifteen, and I was dog-tired. With luck, I told myself, I'd be able to knock off a three-hour nap before showing up for dinner and the new night's round of sexercises.

But I'd forgotten that luck had turned against me. Bad Break Number Three: No sooner had I closed my eyes than there was a knock on my door and Lumombe opened it to admit Su Wing. She said something to him in Belgravian, and he stepped outside. Then she turned to me. "Damon," she said, "you're to discontinue your radio transmissions to Lin Saong. From now on, I'll come to your room every afternoon. You can tell me what you've

132

learned from the nine girls, and I'll convey your messages to Lin Saong." She held out her hand. "Now give me your transmitter."

I gulped. Without the transmitter, I'd really be high and dry. I turned on my sexiest smile. "What's wrong?" I asked. "Doesn't your boss like my broadcasts?"

Her expression told me that the smile hadn't moved her a bit. "You know damned well that she doesn't like your broadcasts. You were told to use the radio only when you had something important to report, and to keep your transmissions as brief as possible. Instead, you've been on the air almost constantly, and you've managed to say enough about PUF's plans that BELSO, if it intercepted your transmissions, would be able to thwart the intended attack.

"Well," I replied pointedly, "if PUF attacks, you'll die along with me. Maybe it wouldn't be such a bad idea if the attack is thwarted."

She sat wearily on the edge of the bed. "I don't want to die, Damon. Not any more than you do. But I have a job to do for my country, and I intend to do it . . . even if I get killed in the process."

I smirked. "Come off it, baby. I might believe that sort of idealistic crap from Lin Saong. But from you I expect a better story. You're no wild-eyed Communist ideologue. You said yourself that the only reason you joined CHILLER was because your beloved country would've executed you as a prostitute if you didn't. Now you expect me to believe that you're ready to give your life for that country?"

She stared at me evenly. "It's not as implausible as it may seem, Damon. Didn't you say that you were coerced into becoming a spy for reasons very similar to the reasons that I was? And haven't you risked your life for your country not just once, but many times?"

"Risked, yes," I admitted. "But if PUF attacks the palace, you won't be just risking your life, you'll be surrendering it. There's a difference between bravery and suicide."

"Maybe so. And maybe not. In any case, PUF won't at-

133

tack if you learn where the bombs are being stored."

"Okay. But they'll still try to dismantle the bombs. And if they fail, you and I'll still go up in the same mushroom cloud."

"That's the chance we've got to take, Damon. Now give me the transmitter."

I shook my head. "That's the chance you've got to take, baby. I'm playing this game for myself—and by my own rules."

Her expression darkened. "I was hoping it wouldn't come to this, Damon, but you leave me no alternative. I must now order you to hand over your radio."

I smirked. "And if I refuse?"

She slowly drew a thirty-eight automatic from underneath her kimono and leveled it at my head.

"If you refuse, Damon, I'll have no choice but to kill you."

I forced a laugh. "Come off it, baby. If you kill me, you'll never find the hidden bombs."

"Maybe not. But at least you won't be able to make any more broadcasts which BELSO can intercept."

I abandoned the laugh, and reverted to my smirk. "You're not worried about BELSO. If you were, you'd never take all the chances you've taken on this caper."

Her eyebrows arched. "What chances, Damon?"

"Like bringing me into the harem under the patently transparent ruse that I'd defected to Red China because the United States wouldn't give me freedom to conduct my sexual experiments. Honey, if sexual freedom was what I was looking for, Red China'd be the last place in the world I'd go looking for it. Do you think Douzi and BELSO don't know this?"

"I think," she replied softly, "that Douzi and BELSO won't suspect your cover story unless you give them reason to suspect it. For example, by sending out transmissions which detail precisely what PUF plans to do and precisely when they plan to do it." Brandishing the gun with one hand, she extended the other toward me. "Now give me the radio, Damon. I'm in no mood to play games."

"No, you're not. At least not now," I said nastily. "But

134

when you and I were together in the car, you were in the mood. Maybe that's why you want the radio. You're afraid I'll tell Su Wing about our hanky-panky together. Your comrades back in Peking would really be happy to hear how you risked detection just so you could get a taste of what you knew I'd be giving to the nine physicists once the show here got on the road."

- "The radio, Damon," she repeated softly, tugging back the hammer of the pistol. "I'm going to count to ten. If the radio isn't in my hand by the time I'm finished, you'll be a dead man."

I forced another laugh. "You're bluffing, baby. If you kill me, you not only blow your only chance to find the hidden bombs, you also blow your scene with Douzi. You're his mistress, remember? How would you explain to him that you happened to be in my room?"

She smiled. "I could say that I came here because your eunuch told me it was a matter of life and death, and that when you got me inside, you tried to rape me." Her smile broadened. "Or I could just leave you dead on the floor. Douzi would never have to know I killed you. Lumombe would cover for me. He dislikes Douzi, and he likes me very much." She took aim with the pistol. "Now I'm going to start counting. You have until ten. One . . . two . . . three . . ."

I suddenly believed that she wasn't bluffing. I wasn't convinced that Douzi would buy either of the explanations she had said she'd give him. But I was convinced that she was convinced, and that was conviction enough for me.

Somewhere in the back of my brain, a line from a popular American magazine ad flashed into being.

The ad read: "Promise her anything, but give her Arpège."

I didn't have any Arpège to give her, but I suddenly could think of a million and one promises.

"Wait, Su Wing!" I said urgently. "If you really want the radio, I'll give it to you. But hear me out first, and see if my idea isn't a better one. I realize it was foolish of me to say so much in my broadcasts. But if I have to relay my information to Lin Saong through you, we'll be wasting

135

valuable time—maybe enough time to make a difference between whether she finds out where the bombs are before PUF attacks. Let me keep the radio. I promise that I won't broadcast anything but essential information. And I promise I won't try anything else that might jeopardize our mission."

"Forget it, Damon," she snapped. "I want the radio, and I want it now. You have until ten. Four . . . five . . . six . . . seven . . ."

I remembered the Arpège ad again, but this time it read a little differently. The wording was: "Promise her anything, but give her a clout."

I'd've liked to give her a clout. The sexy little cutie in the sexy little kimono, who once had seemed so desirable to me, now had lost all her charm. I looked at her and I saw Lin Saong; I saw all the girls from CHILLER; I saw the human female, whom I adored, stripped of everything that was good and sexy and desirable, and reduced to a cold, calculating, emotionless cypher, using sex as a weapon to con more and more people into making it easier and easier for the abominable sexless monster that was Communism to spread its ugly tenacles farther and farther around the globe.

"Eight . . ." she counted. "Nine . . ."

I couldn't give her a clout—not while she had the barrel of her pistol staring me in the face—but maybe, just maybe, I could do something about that pistol.

It was about two feet from my head.

If I grabbed for it, she could fire before my hands got anywhere near it.

But my knees were another matter.

They were directly underneath her gun-hand.

I could jerk them up in a split second, and before she had a chance to realize what was happening, the thirty-eight would be pointing harmlessly at the ceiling.

"Ten . . ." she said, and just as she did, my knees jerked up.

There was an awe-inspiring instant of total silence, then a deafening report, as fire belched from the pistol's barrel and a bullet whiningly crashed into the ceiling.

136

My right hand closed around her wrist. My left closed around the pistol barrel. I jerked the weapon out of her grasp.

Then I did give her a clout—a good, solid backhander. It sent her flying, away from the bed and onto the floor. When she staggered to her knees, a small river of blood had materialized at the corner of her mouth.

I knew it would be far more dangerous to kill her than to let her live. Douzi might buy a cockamamie story from her about how she had killed me because I lured her to my room and tried to rape her. But even at his most gullible he'd never buy any story about why I had killed her, his beloved mistress.

I slowly took the remaining shells from the pistol's chamber. Then I handed the pistol back to Su Wing.

"I'm keeping the radio," I told her. "Now get out of here. You're getting on my nerves."

She nodded, wiped some blood from her mouth, and started silently toward the door. When her hand was on the knob, she turned to face me. "I know that you won't take any orders from me under these circumstances, Damon, but I hope you'll permit me to make a request."

"Go ahead," I scowled.

"Please, please, Damon, don't be so talkative on the radio. I realize that you don't want to die in an attack by PUF. But if BELSO learns that you're spying on Douzi, you'll die anyway—at the hands of executioners far less merciful than the blast of a bomb. I've been tortured by BELSO, Damon, so I know what I'm talking about. They torture slowly . . . painfully . . . so slowly and painfully that a victim of their tortures would accept death a hundred times over in place of just one more minute of torture."

"Thanks for the advice."

"And one thing more, Damon. Please, *please,* don't be so zealous in your quest of Douzi's secrets that you disarm his guards and leave them tied up half-naked in the cabs of armored trucks. Douzi has no reason to suspect right now that it was you who disarmed the guard this morning at the treasury, but you were lucky to get away without getting caught. Please be more careful in the future."

137

I saluted her with one of the bullets I'd emptied from her pistol. My smile told her that I wasn't going to say thanks-for-the-advice more than once.

The corners of her mouth jerked upward in what was half a smile, half an unspoken goodbye. Then she opened the door and walked out, leaving me alone with my thoughts.

Amendment: alone with my thoughts and with Lumombe. The unshakeable eunuch came breezing into the room as soon as she had left.

My thoughts were more interesting to me than he was, so I ignored him and concentrated on them.

So, I mused, nobody knew I was responsible for the fracas at the treasury vault. That was a good sign.

And I had managed very neatly to avoid getting my head blown off by Su Wing's pistol. That was a good sign too.

Maybe my luck had taken an upswing after all.

Or had it?

Now that I thought about it, if my luck were really good, I would've found the bombs in the treasury vault and I wouldn't have had to take the pistol from Su Wing because she never would've pulled it on me!

Nope, I hadn't gotten lucky again yet.

And as developments of the evening later showed, I wasn't about to for quite some time.

When dinner and the social hour were over, I returned to my room to take on the evening's procession of sex-seekers.

Vera, the big-breasted beauty, was first. I gave her the same spiel I had given Tania a few days earlier, and she told me what she knew. Bad Break Number Four: she didn't know anything that Tania hadn't told me already.

Nadia, a brunette named Svetlana, and an Oriental chick named Mai followed in short order. Bad Breaks Numbers Five Through Seven: they couldn't shed any further light on the situation either.

Tania came next. Bad Break Number Eight: she hadn't found out anything new.

After we had made love, I told her about my plan to break the language barrier that separated me from Olga.

138

The plan was simple. In fact, it was so simple that I was kicking myself for not having thought of it earlier.

What is boiled down to was this: Olga dug sex. Ever since the afternoon when I'd given her a sample of my talents on the bench in Douzi's bath, she had delighted in all the little bed-games we have played together. Now, with Tania's help, I was going to invite her to a slightly different kind of bed-game—a game involving three players instead of two. Tania would be the third player, and, as chance would have it, the interpreter who would translate into Russian the questions I wanted to ask Olga, then transate into English the answers she supplied.

"When you see her tomorrow at the laboratory," I told Tania, "tell her what I have in mind. I'm pretty sure she'll like the idea. Then, tomorrow night, both of you come to my room together. Maybe we'll get to the bottom of this crazy business then."

Tania agreed, we made love again, and she left. She promptly was followed by a blonde named Marta, whom I pitched just as I had pitched the other four girls. Bad Break Number Nine: she had nothing to tell me either.

Finally Olga came in for her customary finale. We swung until the nine o'clock curfew, and she left. More tired than I could ever remember being, I dropped off to sleep, and I slept like a baby until seven the following evening, when Lumombe woke me up to tell me it was time to dress for dinner.

I hurried to the dining room, hoping to find out if Tania had set up the threesies shot with Olga. Bad Break Number Ten: Olga had dropped out of sight.

"I spoke to her this morning," Tania reported, "and she was very enthusiastic about the idea of all of us making love together. In fact, she was so enthusiastic that although she hasn't said ten cordial words to me in the past month, she threw her arms around me as though we were intimate friends. She and I agreed that we would come to your room together tonight after the other girls had had their turn. Then we left the laboratory for lunch.

"After lunch, Olga went to Douzi's study—a daily ritual with her—but she never returned to the lab. By five this evening I became concerned. I asked the girls if they had seen her, and they said they hadn't. Finally, when I went to my room to dress, I asked my eunuch to find out from her eunuch where she was. He replied that both she and her eunuch had been driven somewhere by one of the palace chauffeurs. He didn't know where they'd been driven to, but he agreed to question the other eunuchs in an attempt to find out. A few minutes before I came to the dining room he told me what he had learned. The place they'd been driven to was the village of Colon, a small town deep in the Belgravian rain forests, near the Republic of Congo border."

I gulped.

"Are you thinking what I'm thinking?" she asked.

"I'm thinking," I said, "that the bombs are stored in the village of Colon, and that Olga has gone there on very official business."

"You're thinking what I'm thinking," she nodded, her expression very much one of concern.

I thought about it all through the meal. In fact, I thought so much about it that I hardly minded the baked elephant feet—or whatever it was that I was eating. Then, when the meal was over, I made my decision.

"I'm tired of playing sitting duck for PUF, for BELSO and for CHILLER," I told Tania. "I'm going to steal a car and break out of this crazy place. Then I'm going somewhere I can find a telephone, and I'm not coming back until I have half the United States Marine Corps with me. If you'd like to join me, you're welcome to."

"Promise that you'll make love to me while we're waiting for the Marines to land?" she asked.

"I promise."

"Then I'm ready whenever you are."

I waited until Superman and the femme physicists had begun filing into the recreation room. Then, taking Tania's hand, I fell in at the rear of the line.

Connecting the recreation room and the dining room was a small corridor. Midway down the corridor was a door leading to the ground floor of the building. We ducked through the door, down a flight of stairs, along another corridor, into an empty sitting room, through another door and out into the night.

Thanks to my many strolls about the palace grounds during my attempts to out-walk Mazimba and Lumombe, I had learned the layout of the place as well as I knew the layout of my own bedroom. The knowledge now came in handy.

Leaving Tania in a tree-shaded alcove at the intersection of two walking lanes, I hightailed it to my room. There I picked up Lin Saong's transmitter and the gun I had taken from the guard at the treasury building. With these all-important items tucked safely into my pockets, I returned to the alcove.

Then, clutching Tana's hand, I cut across one of the intersecting paths, through a flower garden, down another path, over a small knoll and into the clearing that served as the palace motor pool.

The motor pool was guarded by two armed sentinels. One of them stood alongside the small shack at the entrance, while the other paced around the clearing's perimeter. Crouching behind a canvas-covered truck, I waited for the pacing sentinel to come my way.

He ambled by a few minutes later, his rifle slung over his shoulder, his pith helmet cocked back jauntily atop his head. I let him get past me. Then I sprang from behind the truck, and in one quick motion, I whipped off his helmet with one hand while my other hand brought the butt of the pistol crashing into his skull. He went out like a light.

I took his rifle and tossed it into the seat of the truck, and after whispering some quick instructions to Tania, I cut across the motor pool, crouching low and keeping in the shadows of the neatly parked rows of vehicles.

When I was in place behind the jeep that stood nearest to the other sentinel's shack, I tossed a pebble over my head in Tani's direction. There was a loud *ping!* as it bounced off the roof of a sedan. Then a motor whirred to life, and the canvas-covered truck roared out of its parking place.

The sentinel in the shack came running out of the door as soon as he heard the motor. Tania wheeled the truck

141

down the lane which passed the shack. The sentinel waved his arms frantically for her to stop. She did—about five feet in front of him, just as I had told her to. Unholstering his pistol, he advanced toward her.

I waited until he was a few steps from her door. Then I leaped out from behind the jeep. He turned as I neared him, but his reflexes weren't fast enough. Before he could point his pistol at me, the butt of my pistol cracked into his face. He took a step backward, his eyes rolled skyward and his legs fell out from under him.

I relieved him of his pistol, climbed behind the wheel of the truck and headed for the main gate. About a hundred feet before I would've reached it, I stopped the truck and whispered a few more hasty instructions to Tania. Then I got out, slipped into the woods alongside the road, and carefully worked my way toward the gate guardhouse.

The sentinel in the guardhouse was stretched out in a chair, leafing through a French girlie magazine. I watched through the window as he pored over the pictures, his face a portrait of carnal desire. He looked up when Tania, who had timed my movements, dropped the truck into gear and came rolling down the road. Then, scowling at this interruption of his photovoyeurism, he tossed the book on a desk, stepped out of the guardhouse and waved to her to halt.

By this time I had my routine down so pat that I could've gone through it blindfolded. Once again I sprang out from my hiding place. Once again my arm whistled through the air. Once again my gun butt made contact. One more sentinel bit the dust.

Taking the key ring that was clipped to his belt, I hurried to the gate. The first key I tried didn't fit the lock. Nor did the second. Nor did the third.

I was fumbling with the fourth when I heard a sedan roar around the corner. It turned onto the main road several hundred yards behind the truck. Its headlights gleamed wildy as it bore down toward me.

With feverish fingers I tried the fourth key. It turned the lock. I pushed open the heavy iron gate, then scurried toward the truck.

142

A bullet whistled over my head as I neared the door.
I crouched low and returned fire.
Another whistled by as I reached for the doorhandle.
I pressed my body against the door and returned fire again.
Then there was a third bullet.
Only this one didn't whistle by.
Would you believe, Bad Break Number Eleven?
I felt a numb sensation in my shoulder, and my pistol fell from my hand. "Take off, Tania!" I heard myself yell. Then everything went black.

CHAPTER TEN

I came to in the back seat of a limousine that was speeding along a narrow, winding road. The wound in my shoulder had been crudely bandaged. My wrists were bound behind my back.

Sitting next to me was Tania. Her wrists were bound behind her back also, making her full, round breasts strain against the bodice of her mini-dress like a pair of grapefruits straining against a tight sack. Despite the pain in my shoulder, I couldn't help but glance down at her thighs. The hem of her mini was hiked high, and the warm white flesh of her bare legs gleamed invitingly in the bright moonlight.

In the jumpseat opposite me was my eunuch, Lumombe. He had a pistol trained on my head, and the look in his eyes told me he was just dying to pull the trigger.

In the jumpseat opposite Tania was the pint-sized President of Belgravia himself, Dr. Albert Douzi. He sat with his legs crossed and his arms folded self-satisfiedly across his chest. His eyes were darting back and forth from Tania's legs to my face, as if he were following the ball in a fast-moving ping-poing match. "Ah, Damon," he beamed when he noticed that my eyes were open, "you've rejoined the land of the living."

I managed a weak smile. "Better aim next time, Doctor."

He chuckled. "It wasn't a question of poor aim, Damon. It was a question of not killing a goose that might lay a golden egg."

"You can thank me for that, Damon," came a voice from the front seat. "I pointed out to Dr. Douzi how you'd

144

be much more valuable to him alive than dead."

I didn't have to look to identify the speaker. It was Su Wing. Douzi winced at the interruption—not much, but just enough so that I could see he thought she should keep her pretty little mouth shut.

"To whom would I be more valuable, baby?" I challenged, exploiting the situation's possibilities for stirring up internal strife. "To him . . . or to you?"

"How could you possibly be valuable to me?" she asked edgily, apparently not realizing that she was getting herself in deeper with every word.

"The same way I was valuable every other time you felt the need for sexual servicing," I grinned. "And don't try to deny it, because Tania here is a witness." I nudged Tania's knee with my thigh. "Remember the time you came to my room, honey, and found Su Wing and me making love?"

"Which time was that?" my pretty seatmate purred with deliciously feigned innocence. "The time you were doing it in bed, or the time you were doing it standing against the wall?"

There was a pregnant silence. Then Douzi chuckled softly. "Clever psychology on your part, Damon, trying to create animosity between Su Wing and me. But it won't work. She already warned me you might try something like this."

I grinned evilly and stared him straight in the eye. "Did she also warn you that PUF plans to attack your palace a week from now?"

His chuckle was louder. "As a matter of fact, she did—three days ago." Then, suddenly, he stopped chuckling. "But how did *you* know about the attack?"

"He knew, darling, because he was the person my so-called comrades chose to deliver the message to me," she put in quickly. "He told me the day he arrived at the palace, and I told you the very same night."

"Why would they choose me to deliver the message?" I shot back. "According to the timetable, I was supposed to be in the palace when the attack took place."

Douzi scratched his head. "This is getting very confusing. Damon, if you were supposed to be in the palace when the attack took place, why didn't you simply refuse to come to the palace?"

"Because," I ad-libbed, "I didn't know about the attack until after I had arrived at the palace. Su Wing told me about it after the first time she and I made love, and she promised to get me out of the palace with her because she didn't want to lose my services as a lover."

"He's lying, dearest," she rebutted. "He came to the palace knowing that the attack would take place because he had been promised that both he and I would be rescued before it actually did."

I tried to put myself in Douzi's shoes as the person who had to decide which of the two stories was true. I decided that I'd think twice before I accepted either of them.

Douzi didn't think twice. "Nice try, Damon," he said, smirking. "But you don't fool me. I'm onto your game."

"What's my game?" I asked.

"You want desperately to save your skin, and you're saying anything that comes to your mind in the hope that I'll believe you and turn against Su Wing."

"Okay, have it your own way. But don't say I didn't warn you when a battalion of PUF stormtroopers busts in on your little meeting at Colon."

He bolted upright in his seat. "What do you know about Colon?"

"Why not ask Su Wing? She's the one who told me."

His eyes narrowed. "She couldn't have told you, Damon, because I never told her." He swallowed hard. "Now what do you know?"

I suddenly remembered the transmitter in my hip pocket, and the thought occurred to me that it might not be a bad idea to put out conversation on the airwaves, where Walrus-moustache's radio man might intercept it. Maneuvering my hands behind me on the seat, I flicked on the switch.

"I know a great deal, Douzi," I said, extra-loud so that the tiny transistor mike would be sure to pick up every word. "I know all about your bombs and how you developed them. I know what you plan to do with them now that they are developed. And I know a lot more. Also,

146

I'm not the only person who knows. The United States government is on to your plans, and they've got a regiment of Marines in your country just waiting to pounce on you when I give the word."

"A regiment of Marines?" gulped Su Wing.

"Yep," I smirked, playing my part to the hilt, "a regiment of Marines." Tania, of course, knew that I was bluffing, but her expression said that she'd known about the Marines all along. Douzi and Su Wing were staring at me wide-eyed.

"You see, Su Wing," I went on, "my country might make a mistake now and then, but it never makes the same mistake twice. We made a mistake in Vietnam when we let you Commie creeps work almost without interference at building the National Liberation Front and its military arm, the Vietcong, into a crack fighting force. So when you started trying the same stunt here in Belgravia with the Peoples' United Front, we stepped in fast. PUF headquarters had been under surveillance by our intelligence people for more than a year now, and so has CHILLER. We've been careful not to let you know about our presence—so careful that we smuggled the Marines across the Republic of Congo border in groups of five and six over a period of eight months. But now we're here in full force, and we're all ready to swing into action. Let PUF make one false move, or let Douzi's nationalist army make one false move, and we step in for the kill." For emphasis, I flashed a scowl that Chesty Puller would've been proud of.

Both Douzi and Su Wing stared at me silently for a moment. Then Su Wing smiled, and her eyes lit up as if she had suddenly been struck with divine inspiration. "You're bluffing, Damon. Back at the palace you were worried stiff about the PUF attack. That's why you were on the radio all the time, making those crazy broadcasts to Lin Saong. You wanted to let BELSO know what was happening so that they could take action against PUF before . . . PUF . . . stormed . . . the . . . palace." The end of her sentence trailed into near-nothingness and her expression froze as she realized what a damaging admission she had just made.

Douzi appeared dumbstruck. His eyes had a faraway

look, and the corners of his mouth were quivering. Then, very slowly, he pulled himself together. "Radio broadcasts, Su Wing?" he asked quietly and with elaborate sarcasm. "How does it happen that a man whom you brought into my harem solely to entertain the girls was making radio broadcasts."

"I—it was something I d-didn't know about," she stammered. "I—I—I had been led to believe he had come only to entertain the girls. But CH-CHILLER had assigned him a spy mission without telling me."

"Oh?" replied the diminutive dictator, his sarcasm thickening. "And how did it happen that CHILLER, of which you claim to be the commander, took such an action without consulting you?"

"I—I—" she said. Then the words froze on her lips. She stared straight ahead, and said nothing.

"Pig!" spat Douzi. His tiny arm lashed out, and his fist caught her square in the jaw, knocking her against the dashboard. She righted herself, and the arm lashed out again. The blow landed on her temple, and she staggered against the door window. This time she knew better than to come back for more. While Douzi glared at her, she simply cowered there, her arms crossed across her face protectively, her body shaking with deep sobs.

Douzi glared for a moment more, then turned to me. "I think, Damon," he said softly, "that you have some explaining to do."

I could, of course, have told him to go to hell, but the transmitter in my hip pocket was still beaming our conversation through the airwaves—and hopefully into the receiver of one of Walrus-moustache's men. I wanted to get as much of the story on record as I could.

It was quite a story.

When I first came to Douzi's palace, I had never dreamed that it would be as simple as it was.

But that was because I was then thinking as a spy rather than as a sexologist.

Then, as I lay in bed one morning bemoaning my inability to break the language barrier with Olga, I had begun thinking as a sexologist, and I had hypothesized that

148

Douzi didn't have a bomb after all.

The hypothesis was off base, but many of the conclusions which it helped me form about Douzi were deadly accurate.

Now, as we rode in his limousine to a rendezvous in the border village of Colon, I was thinking as both a spy and a sexologist, and every last piece of the crazy puzzle fit into place.

"Douzi," I said, "you made the one fatal mistake that a man of your intelligence and background should never make. You committed the unforgivable sin. You broke the one rule that no successful politician ever breaks."

He looked at me questioningly. "Which mistake, Damon? Which sin? Which rule?"

I grinned. "There's an old Yiddish saying that describes it in a nutshell. Translated loosely, it says: you don't eat in the bathroom."

His brow furrowed. "I don't follow you."

My grin broadened. "Let me put it this way. There're only two ways a man can successfully mix business and pleasure. The first is to make your business a pleasure, and the second is to make your pleasure a business. The latter is what I've done, and it's worked out just fine. The former is what a lot of other people have done, and that's worked out fine too. But you, Douzi, didn't do either. You made sex your pleasure and politics your business, and then you tried to mix them. And it just didn't work."

"It's been working just fine so far."

"Apparently, yes. Actually, no. And that's why your world is now about to topple down around your ears. You're through, Douzi—finished. And because I'm in a talkative mood, I'll tell you exactly how your downfall came about."

I told him—not because I was in a talkative mood, but because I wanted the whole story beamed out over the airwaves. I began with his trip to Europe, and his decision to study psychiatry because he thought it would help him solve his sexual problems. I then went into his return to Belgravia, his assumption of leadership in the country's independence movement, his election to the Belgravian

149

presidency and his construction of the palace.

I had been just making calculated guesses when I first came up with these thoughts while pursuing the hypothesis that he wasn't involved in a program of nuclear bomb building. But as I told the story to Douzi, I knew that I wasn't guessing; I was stating facts. The expression on his face told me that my confidence in my deductions wasn't at all unjustified.

"After the palace was built," I continued, extending the implications of the facts to their logical conclusions, and working in the other bits and pieces of information I had picked up along the line, "you grew restive. You had stocked your harem with all sorts of native girls and boys, but they weren't satisfying you sexually. What you wanted was some outside action, some high-quality action, some of the action which you had lusted after but never achieved while you were in Europe. Not that there was anything inferior about the native sexmates you held prisoner. But to you, Douzi, they seemed inferior, because deep down you're a racist. Not a racist who says 'black is best,' but a racist who says 'white is best,' or 'yellow is best'—more precisely, a racist who says 'anything *but* black is best.' In Europe, where you were rejected by white girls whom you desired, you grew to resent your blackness—and you grew to resent your diminutive stature. The fact that these girls rejected you made you want them all the more. And since you couldn't change your skin pigmentation or your size so that the girls would want you, you rummaged about for a plan which would enable you to make them have to take you as you were."

He nodded sadly. "Your talent for psychiatric deduction is extraordinary, Damon. I've pondered the matter at great and painful length, and I must confess that I agree with you completely."

"Non-black girls weren't the only forbidden fruit you lusted after," I continued. "You also lusted after the forbidden fruit of world political power. In Europe, you saw firsthand what that power is like. You lived in England and in France. You saw Churchill and deGaulle, Franco and Hitler. Then you came back to Belgravia and were elected

150

to the presidency of a nation which most people never heard of, let alone respected. You enjoyed almost absolute power here at home, but in the world community you were a cypher. Belgravia had a seat in the United Nations, but its voice was swallowed up among thousands of other voices. You wanted to change all that. You wanted to become another Churchill, another deGaulle. And you knew that the only way you could do it was if Belgravia became as powerful as England and France—or Russia, or Red China, or the United States. To become that powerful, Belgravia needed nuclear capabilities."

"Right again, Damon," he confessed. "I won't deny it."

I smiled self-satisfiedly and plunged on. "So there you were with two enormous unfulfilled desires. They tormented your every waking moment, and they haunted your dreams. And then, one day, you got an idea. A crazy idea, it seemed at first, then a not-so-crazy idea. It was an idea which you thought would enable you to satisfy both your desires in one fell swoop. You did some research and you decided that you might just be able to pull it off. Then you went ahead with it. Tapping the Belgravian treasury for funds, you hired private detectives to find you some nuclear physicists—not just ordinary nuclear physicists, nuclear physicists who (a) were female, (b) were beautiful, (c) were tinged with sexual scandal of some sort and (d) lived in one or another of the Communist bloc countries. Your plan was to lure these physicists to Belgravia to lecture at your National University, then, once they were here, to entice them into working on your nuclear development program in exchange for the sexual services of Superman, or if that wasn't enticement enough, in fear of having their scandals exposed for refusing to work for you. What the girls never were told—and what probably none of them ever expected—was that once they had developed your bomb you intended to keep them prisoner and force them to offer you the same sexual services which Superman had offered them."

I felt Tania stiffen alongside me. "I can understand how you deduced that he wanted us to work on his nuclear program," she said. "But how did you know he planned to

151

keep us prisoner after the bomb was developed."

"At first," I admitted, "I didn't. But when I weighed all the factors against Douzi's personality as I now know it, I could see that there was no other possibility. You see, if he was interested only in developing a bomb, he would have had no reson to recruit only beautiful females for the project. He could have made his job a lot simpler by recruiting males and offering them sexual services, or even by recruiting persons of both sexes and setting up harems for the men while Superman was entertaining the girls. But Douzi wanted more than just a bomb. As the saying goes, he wanted to eat in the bathroom. So he limited his recruiting to beautiful girls—girls he would enjoy sexually himself after their work was done. He said nothing of these plans before the bomb was developed and he made no attempt to have sex with any of the girls, because he was afraid that it might interfere with the project. But now that the bomb has been perfected, he can admit freely what he had in mind."

Douzi smiled broadly. "I admit it, Damon. But I believe you've made something of a grammatical error. Didn't you just speak of something I 'had' in mind, 'had' being the past tense. I suggest you change that to the present tense and speak of what I *have* in mind?"

"Aren't you forgetting about my Marines?" I reminded him.

He chuckled. "Where are your Marines, Damon?" He made a big production of looking around the car. "I don't see them anywhere."

"They're around," I said, wishing I could believe it. "They're just waiting for the word to pounce on you."

"And who's going to give them the word, Damon? Surely not you. In case you've forgotten, you're my prisoner. The man who's sitting across from you has a pistol trained on your head. A few minutes from now, this car will stop at a cabin on the outskirts of the village of Colon. Olga, the chief of my laboratory staff, is waiting there now. In her possession is a compound which was synthesized today in the lab. It's a compound the discovery of

152

which has solved the riddle of how to develop the super-bomb we've been planning. Once I arrive at the cabin, she will demonstrate with a miniature explosion—an explosion involving sub-microscopic particles—that the theory which was worked out in the lab can in fact be applied with actual chemical elements. When this has been accomplished, the formula for the compound will be handed over to my plant in Colon where the actual bombs are being manufactured. I anticipate that it it will take twenty-four hours to complete the first of these bombs by incorporating the compound, and twenty-four hours more to ship it down the river to Port duBeers. There it will be loaded on an airplane, taken out over the South Atlantic, and dropped. After it has been exploded, my representative at the United Nations will identify Belgravia as the nation which perfected it. He will also reveal that Belgravia now possesses a sufficient store of similar bombs to blow up the entire world—an assertion which, when he makes it, will be true, since two such bombs, at full strength, will be enough to do the job. Belgravia then will be recognized as a world power, a power which can hold its own with Russia, Red China, the United States and all the others. Now tell me, what use will your Marines be when that happens?"

"Don't be surprised," I said softly, "if they show up before it happens."

His chuckle blossomed into a full-blown laugh. "I'll be very surprised, Damon. Very surprised."

The limousine slowed down as we approached the crest of a hill. Then it turned into a dirt road. A few minutes later, it pulled to a halt in front of a small stone cabin. The guard on the porch snapped to a stiff position of attention. The eunuch who had been serving as Douzi's chauffeur opened the car doors, and our entire party trooped inside.

The interior of the cabin was one large room. Set up on a table which ran the length of one of the walls was an immense metal contraption that looked like it belonged in a Dr. Frankenstein movie. Next to the contraption was a cluster of vials, tubes, beakers and aluminum boxes. Olga was sitting nearby, flanked by two more armed guards, one

153

of which was her eunuch. Five black-skinned men in business suits sat in animated conversation at a coffee table opposite her.

Everyone rose in deference to Douzi, and the men rushed over to shake his hand. He greeted them warmly, then gestured toward me and Tania. "Gentlemen," he announced, "we have some unexpected visitors. The man is a United States spy, who assures me that his country has a regiment of Marines just waiting to attack us. The girl is one of my physicists, who had the misfortune to be in his company when he was apprehended trying to escape through the palace's main gate. Dr. Rod Damon and Dr. Tania Pavlofsky, permit me to introduce the chairman and his four associates on Belgravia's nuclear weapons development committee—Dr. William Baio, Dr. Samuel Salukka, Dr. Hayden Messavutu, Mr. Arthur Grina and Mr. David Hotoso."

The men muttered surprised greetings to us. Then the chairman, Dr. Baio, stepped forward and nervously cleared his throat. "Forgive us, Mr. President, if we fail to conceal our astonishment, but we had not anticipated that you would invite guests to the proceedings." If I read the good doctor's eyes carefully, what he was really saying to Douzi was, What the hell did you bring these geeks here for?

Douzi smiled. "It was not my intention to invite guests, gentlemen. But as I told you in our telephone conversation this afternoon, the compound which has just been discovered appears to be the answer to all our problems. Naturally I am eager to get our program off the ground as soon as possible. That's why, when I learned of the compound, I didn't send a formula up here by messenger for routine testing but instead had lovely Olga bring the ingredients here personally. At my command, she will mix the necessary amount, and you will bring it to the test site in the garden. Then I shall watch personally as you detonate the microscopic sample. The miniature blast will herald the beginning of a great new era for us and for our nation." He turned toward Tania and me, as if he had just remembered that Baio's comment about us was what set him spieling in the first place. "As for our guests, it is unfortunate that

154

they must be here to share the glorious moment with us. However, they were captured minutes before I had left the palace to come here. A guard from the motor pool, whom Damon earlier had disarmed, stopped them just as they were heading out the main gate in a truck. I would've left them back at the palace, but frankly Damon has proved to be quite a tricky fellow. I don't want to let him out of my sight for one minute until our delegate at the UN has made his speech and I know for sure that Damon can do no further harm to our program."

"It would seem, sir," suggested the ever-diplomatic Baio, "that a man who is so dangerous might more advantageously be killed than held prisoner."

"Perhaps," Douzi nodded. "But Damon is quite the clever boy, and I think I can find a useful spot for him in my administration after Belgravia has been granted world recognition."

Baio's eyes widened, as did the eyes of the four other committee members, as did Su Wing's, as did Olga's, as did Tania's, and as especially did mine.

But I didn't let the flattery go to my head. "What do you have in mind, buddy?" I wisecracked. "Castrating me and appointing me chief eunuch?"

He smiled the smile of one too sure of his ground to let the impropitious remarks of a flunky disturb him. "Let's just keep that a mystery for now, Damon. Suffice it to say that a man with your sexual knowledge could prove extremely useful to me."

I forced a laugh that sounded a lot more confident than it was. "Wait until my Marines get here, half-pint. They'll mop the floor with you creeps."

His smile broadened. "Ah yes, Damon, your Marines. What's the old saying—if wishes were horses, beggars would ride?"

I tried to think of a snappy comeback, but I couldn't.

Then suddenly I didn't have to.

The sound effects department took care of everything for me.

The sound: a pistol shot followed by the thud of a body on the cabin porch.

Douzi and the five committeemen took cover behind a couch. Lumombe and another eunuch rushed out the door, their pistols at the ready.

The sound effects department swung back into action, this time with a burst of machine gun fire.

More astonished than anyone, I summoned the bravado to call out, "The Marines have landed!" Then I crouched with Tania in a corner of the room and wondered who the hell was doing the shooting and how they got here.

From outside came the voice of a woman. She shouted something in Belgravian. I couldn't make out any of the words except one. It was Douzi's name.

Douzi shouted something back, and there was another burst of machine gun fire. The bullets zinged across the entire front of the building, shattering the windows and tearing through the door.

The woman shouted something else, and Douzi, knees shaking, started for the porch, his hands raised over his head.

Tania supplied me with a translation. "The woman outside said that the house is surrounded, and that unless Douzi surrenders it will be blown up."

The room was silent as the diminutive dictator opened the door and walked outside. I heard the scuffling of feet going through shrubbery, then climbing the stairs. Then Douzi came back into the room, his hands still over his head. He was followed by three girls. One held a pistol against his back. The other two had submachine guns cradled in their arms.

"The Marines, Damon?" beamed Su Wing. "You mean the girls from CHILLER."

And that's who it was, all right. The girl with the pistol was Lin Saong. The two with the submachine guns were Girl Number One and Girl Number Two, with whom I'd enjoyed that round of sex games people play.

"Don't anyone move or Dr. Douzi is a dead man," Lin Saong told us. "Su Wing, collect their weapons."

The weapons were collected. Then Douzi, the committeemen, the one surviving eunuch, Olga, Tania and I were herded to the center of the room.

156

In the process, I managed to catch Lin Saong's eye. "Admit it, baby, I did a great job. You picked up my radio beacon, and you followed it all the way to paydirt. Do I get the Chairman Mao Citation for Valor, or do I have to settle for Honorable Mention."

She said something in Chinese to Su Wing and the girls with the submachine guns. Then she favored me with a nasty grin. "Your transmissions, Damon, proved extremely valuable to us—even though that wasn't your intention. I listened to your broadcast while my comrades and I were driving from Port duBeers to here, and I found it most enlightening. Now, please sit on the floor with the rest of the nice people and permit Su Wing to tie you up. I've radioed the nearest detatchment of PUF troops, and they'll be here in a couple of hours to collect this splendid aggregation of prisoners. While we're waiting for them, we can pass the time listening to your account of how you uncovered the rest of Douzi's secrets."

As if on cue, Su Wing grabbed the ropes which had bound my wrists all during the ride from the palace. Tugging me toward her, she slipped another rope through them. The new rope, I could see, ran through the wrist-ropes of everyone else in the party. We were all being seated in a circle in the center of the floor, our backs facing each other, our bonds connecting us in a neatly goemetric daisy-chain.

"Wait a minute," I told Lin Saong. "I'm on your side. I'm the guy who solved the mystery for you. Why are you tying me up?"

She chuckled. "Don't flatter yourself, Damon. You didn't solve the mystery. We still don't know exactly where the bombs are stored. We'll find out, of course. But now that we've captured Douzi, there won't be any need to disarm them. When the PUF troops arrive, they'll take Douzi with them. One of the problems with an autocratic government is that it lends itself very facilely to being overthrown. What you've just seen is a *coup d'etat*. Douzi's captors, the Peoples' United Front, now need only move into the palace and take over the reigns of government—and the bombs."

157

"Okay, hurray for PUF," I said. "But you still haven't answered my question. I'm on your side. Why are you tying me up?"

"We're tying you up, Damon," she said evenly, "because the PUF troops will bring you back to the palace with Douzi. When the coup is announced, PUF will also reveal that an agent of the United States government—namely, one Dr. Rod Damon—worked hand in hand with Douzi and his fascist regime to develop the bomb. I needn't tell you what this revelation will mean in terms of world opinion against the United States."

"And I needn't tell you, Lin Saong," I replied, "that of all the good-for-nothing double-crossing broads I've met in my life, you take the crocheted loving cup."

She laughed. "What is the American expression, Damon? 'Sticks and stones will break my bones, but names will never hurt me.' But let's not bicker. You were telling a very interesting story in the car. And you stopped at just the point where you were about to reveal what happened after you infiltrated the Belgravian harem. Please continue."

158

CHAPTER ELEVEN

I wasn't really in a storytelling mood.

But my arms were tied behind my back, I was bound to Douzi and the other prisoners, and two CHILLER-chicks with submachine guns at the ready were staring me straight in the face.

Somewhere in the back of my head, a light bulb with "idea" written over it flashed to life. It was an idea about how I might just possibly escape before the PUF troops arrived to bring me back to the palace.

I wasn't sure it'd work. In fact, the odds against its working were formidable. But it was the only chance I had. And to pull it off I had to put the CHILLER chicks in the proper frame of mind. Storytelling, I suddenly realized, might just be the perfect way to do it.

"When Douzi welcomed me to the palace," I said, "he accepted completely Su Wing's explanation that I had defected to Red China because the United States wouldn't give me enough freedom to conduct my sexual experiments. He also accepted without question her claim that Red China had sent me to Belgravia at her request. It was a wholly implausible explanation, and I couldn't for the life of me figure out why he had bought it. Eventually I decided that he had bought it because he wasn't working on a nuclear development program after all. Only if there were no program, I reasoned, would he be so unsuspecting. But then, thanks to Tania and the other physicists, I got virtually incontrovertible evidence that he was working on the program. I then guessed that Su Wing had double-crossed CHILLER. If she had, I reasoned, she and Douzi might be planning together for the day when the bomb would be developed and Belgravia would become a world power. Under these circumstances, he would have known that my story was false, but he wouldn't have been concerned, because he would have believed that I'd be helpless to do anything to stop him. I was convinced that this hunch was right when Su Wing came to my room and tried to take my radio transmitter from me. I figured that she wanted the transmitter because she wanted to prevent me from revealing to Lin Saong anything which might disrupt her plans. But this line of reasoning was all wet too. As tonight's events have shown, Su Wing is very much a loyal Communist. The only reason she wanted the transmitter was because she was afraid BELSO would monitor my broadcasts. And that left me with the original question: Why had Douzi accepted her explanation?"

"He accepted it," interrupted Lin Saong, "because, fascist pig that he is, he was so eager to develop his bomb that he lost all his common sense."

"Wrong," I replied. "He lost his common sense all right. But not out of eagerness to develop his bomb. As I pointed out earlier, he's suffered all his life from rejection by girls whom he finds desirable—Caucasian girls, Oriental girls, all girls except native Belgravian pygmy girls. As President of Belgravia, and probably earlier in Europe, he unquestionably hired prostitutes. But while they gratified him physically, they did nothing at all for his ego, which was the one part of him that really needed gratification. Still, he couldn't resign himself to accepting girls of his own size and race. Consequently when BELSO picked up Su Wing and Douzi learned about it, he wanted to have sexual intercourse with her. And when she, eager to infiltrate his harem, pretended that she really found him sexually satisfying, he was so pleased that he made her his mistress—this despite the fact that common sense should have told him he couldn't dare risk having an acknowledged enemy agent anywhere near his palace."

"You're right, Damon," Su Wing put in. "The little worm really was enchanted with me. You should have seen him when we made love. I'd pretend that I was having orgasm, and he'd be beside himself with glee. Actually the
160

only times I did have orgasm while I was at the palace was when you made love to me in the car."

I glanced out of the corner of my eye at Douzi. He sat in a posture of total defeat, his tiny shoulders hunched, his eyes riveted to the floor.

"Yes," I said, suddenly feeling a surge of pity for the diminutive dictator, "he was enchanted with you. Not enchanted enough that he gave you *carte blanche* to the physicists' laboratory or that he told you where his bombs were stored. But enchanted enough that he welcomed me to the palace on your recommendation. And that fit perfectly into Red China's plans."

"China's plans?" asked Tania, ever the ideal straight man. "What were they?"

"China's main goal," I replied, "was to prevent Belgravia from becoming a nuclear power, because China knew that if Douzi's regime achieved the world stature it sought, PUF's chances of taking over the government would be nonexistent. It was for that reason that China volunteered to work along with the United States, Russia and the other nuclear powers in foiling Douzi's bomb development program. Then, when the United States sent me to Belgravia, China saw an opportunity to achieve additional goals it never before had dreamed of achieving. By arranging things so that I was in Douzi's palace when PUF attacked, China would be able to blame the United States for the bomb program which Douzi actually had set up on his own."

I turned to Lin Saong. "You knew," I told her, "that the bombs which already had been developed weren't stored anywhere on the palace grounds. And so did Su Wing know it. That's why she wasn't at all concerned about PUF's attacking the palace. But you told me that the bombs were there because you wanted to spur me into working faster. You figured that I might just be lucky enough to find out where they were, which would make PUF's job a lot easier when the coup was staged. And if I didn't find out, you'd've lost nothing. PUF still would stage its coup, and Douzi's government would fall into China's hands, assuming that he didn't perfect his bomb and make his play at the United

161

Nations before the coup could be staged. That, by the way—the play at the United Nations, which you suspected all along that he would make—was the real reason for your haste."

"And I almost succeeded," said Douzi in a small voice. "I was just inches away from success."

"Yes," I confessed, "you were. And you would have succeeded except for two reasons: (a) the physicists in your harem liked me, and (b) your eunuchs disliked you."

"My eunuchs?" he asked, surprised. "How they fit into the picture."

"It was Olga's eunuch, Douzi, who told Tania's eunuch that you were coming here to Colon tonight. And it was Tania who told me. When I found out, it was my intention to escape from the palace, make contact with the United States and lead a military mission here to seize your bomb storage facilities. As things happened, you made my job easier than that. When your men caught me trying to escape the palace, you brought me here with you. My radio transmitter was broadcasting to Lin Saong during our entire ride in your limousine. All she had to do was follow the beacon."

"And all because of a loose-mouthed cur," he growled, glowering at Olga's eunuch. "I took these vermin in off the streets. They were starving, and I fed them until they were fat. And what for? So they could turn against me."

"Why shouldn't they turn against you?" I shot back, smiling. My previous feeling of sympathy for him now was completely gone. "Sure, you fed them until they were fat. But you deprived them of their manhood. You turned them into sexless creatures who could never again think of themselves as fully human. And why did you do it? You did it, Douzi, because your own warped ego demanded it. You yourself felt sexually inadequate, and to compensate for these feelings of inadequacy, you surrounded yourself with men who were totally sexless. Worse yet, you subjected the poor creatures to the most degrading forms of sexual submission—like the undressing ritual and the acts of fellatio which I observed at your bath. Every time you put a eunuch through these tortures, you felt better, because you knew that as bad off as you were sexually you were still a lot better off than the eunuch was."

"Mr. President," said Dr. Baio, completely aghast, "is this true?"

"It's true," I snapped. "And there's a lot more to the twisted sexual personality of your leader than just that. Douzi not only humiliated the eunuchs, he also forced them to entertain him sexually—and he enjoyed their attentions immensely. He was also a leather fetishist, as I learned when I saw him nibbling on Su Wing's leather dress at the bath. In fact, I'd be kind of surprised to learn that there was a sexual perversion he *didn't* practice."

"He was a sadist too, Damon," Su Wing continued. "Why do you think you've never seen me wearing anything but high-necked kimonos and tunics. My arms and legs are unmarked, but my back and breasts and abdomen are completely covered with scars from his whippings."

"I thought," said Douzi weakly, "that you enjoyed being whipped. You certainly seemed to enjoy it."

I saw that the conversation was shaping up exactly as I wanted it to—exactly as it had to if I was going to put my farfetched escape plan into effect. "She pretended she enjoyed it," I said quickly, "just like she pretended she enjoyed everything else you did. But actually she despised it, just like she despised you and everything about you."

"That's right, Damon," said Su Wing, playing right into my hand. "I despised him like I've never despised anyone in my life. Not once during my years as a prostitute in Peking did I encounter any man who revolted me more—or who was more of a sexual washout."

I played my trump card. "What a shame," I mused, "that we have to turn this louse over to PUF before we can subject him to some of the same humiliations that you and so many other people suffered at his hands. A creep like him ought to be paid back in his own coin."

For a moment the room was silent. I glanced from Lin Saong to Su Wing to Girl Number One to Girl Number Two. Lin Saong's face was impassive, but Su Wing wore an expression of mischievous delight, and Girls Number One and Two were looking at me with their old sexual hunger showing.

"What are you getting at, Damon?" Lin Saong asked finally.

I grinned noncommitally, and said nothing.

"I think," supplied Su Wing, her eyes glowing brightly, "that Damon means that Douzi deserves a dose of his own medicine."

Lin Saong's brow furrowed. "And how does he propose that the dose be administered?"

Su Wing looked to me.

My grin broadened, and I nodded.

"Perhaps," said Su Wing, "we might humiliate Douzi sexually right here—by forcing him to watch Damon make love to me."

Lin Saong frowned, as if the idea was totally repulsive. But her eyes betrayed an inner desire. "It would be"—she paused—"highly unorthodox."

"True," said Su Wing, beaming as if she was imagining the act actually taking place. "But there's no reason why it couldn't be done. The PUF troops won't be here for at least another hour. We've got nothing else to do while we wait for them."

Lin Saong's frown deepened. But her feelings evidently were ambivalent, because the desire in her eyes became more pronounced. "I don't object to sexual indulgence when it's necessary to accomplish a mission," she said, as if talking to herself. "But, in this case, our mission already is accomplished, and the sex act would serve only to gratify the participants. As we both know, that's diametrically opposed to the thinking of Chairman Mao."

My eyes found those of Su Wing. I tried to remind her, via mental telepathy, that she'd soon be going back to Red China, where it might be many moons before she got another opportunity to enjoy the pleasures which Chairman Mao was so violently against.

Evidently the message got across. "Under these circumstances," she told Lin Saong, "Chairman Mao might very well approve. After all, would we not be demonstrat-

164

ing to this capitalist swine that we Communists are capable of beating him at his own game?"

The go-lights in Lin Saong's eyes were glowing more brightly than ever. Her frown vanished. "You have a point," she said. Then, turning to me, she asked, "Would you consent to participating in such a venture, Damon?"

I smiled blandly. "Madame Saong, I'm an agent of the United States government, and as such I'm not at all interested in demonstrating that you Commie creeps can beat us capitalist swine at our own game."

Her frown flashed on again. Su Wing looked at me with an expression of utter bewilderment.

"However," I added quickly, "I *am* your prisoner, and if you order me at gunpoint to stage such a demonstration, I'll have little choice but to acquiesce."

Lin Saong's frown was replaced by an expectant smile. Su Wing was so caught up with enthusiasm that her hips involuntarily took up a slow gyrating motion.

"Furthermore," I grinned, "if you really want to make Douzi suffer, I'd suggest that you don't stop with my merely making love to Su Wing. Why not go for broke and stage a spectacle that'll *really* humiliate him, one that'll demonstrate his sexual inadequacy all the more forcefully."

It was a lousy trick to play, even on a crumb like Douzi. But it was my only hope for escape.

"What sort of spectacle do you have in mind, Damon?" asked Lin Saong and Su Wing in eager unison.

I assumed a thoughtful pose. "Well, let's see. If it would humiliate him to watch me making love to his former mistress, it would humiliate him twice as much to see me making love to both his former mistress and her commanding officer."

My face became animated.

"And, as humiliating as this would be, he'd be even more humiliated if I satisfied four girls instead of two. We could add the two girls with the machine guns, couldn't we?"

I now was grinning like a bastard.

"And to really rub it in, suppose we untie the two Russian physicists, Tania and Olga, and have them whip him with belts while he's being forced to watch us?"

Su Wing looked like a little girl who just discovered a brand spankin' new bicycle under her Christmas tree. Lin Saong was only a shade less exuberant.

I glanced sideways at Tania. She was exuberant too, but I hoped it was for a different reason.

"Well," I prodded Lin Saong, "what do you think?"

A shadow of doubt seemed to cloud her face. "I don't know," she said uncertainly, "if I could lend myself to such an enterprise. You see, Damon, I'm—I'm—"

I waited, almost sure of what she would say.

"I'm a virgin."

"All the better!" I cheered. "Imagine how humiliated Douzi will be when he realizes that the commander of CHILLER is sacrificing her maidenhood just to rub his face in the mud."

"Well—" She hesitated. Then, a suspicious smile taking form on her lips, she said, "But, Damon, if all four of us girls are making love to you, there'll be no one to guard the prisoners."

"They'll still be tied up," I reminded her. "They couldn't possibly get away."

"Yes. But you wouldn't be tied up. You could get away."

"Are you kidding? While I'm making love to four girls at the same time? I may be a contortionist, honey, but I'm not a magician."

Her nod said that the point was well taken. But the look in her eyes told me that she still was entertaining a few doubts.

I decided to try a little psychology. It was a risky move, I knew. But unless I misread the signals, Lin Saong was really dying for an excuse to have a go with me. I usually don't misread signals—not where sex is concerned.

"Well," I said, crossing my fingers behind my back for luck, "if the only thing that's stopping you is your fear that I might escape, you can always cut yourself out of the deal and hold your gun on us while we do our tricks."

I waited for her answer. She hesitated. Then the corners of her mouth slowly inched upward in an expectant smile that displayed her pretty white teeth to full advantage. "Okay, Damon," she said, "you've convinced me. I'll sacrifice my virginity to help rub the face of this capitalist swine in the mud." She gestured for Su Wing to untie me. "Now precisely what sort of sexual coupling do you have in mind?"

I smiled, very much relieved. "Do you remember back in Port duBeers when I demonstrated what the author of *Hikatsu-sho* described as The Position of The Mysterious Pearl and The Two Crabs?"

She panted expectantly. "I do."

"Let's just call this one The Position of The Mysterious Pearl, The Beast With Two Backs, and The Two Daggers in Their Scabbards."

Her eyebrows arched quizzically. "How is it performed?"

"Untie Douzi and the two Russian girls. Then take off your clothes and I'll show you."

Douzi and the two Russian girls were untied. Then I supervised as the miniature madman who once ruled Belgravia was undressed, and his ankles and feet were tightly bound. Tania and Olga relieved two of the Belgravian committeemen of their belts. Then Douzi's body was draped across a chair, from which he'd have an unobstructed view of The Position of The Mysterious Pearl, The Beast With Two Backs, and The Two Daggers in Their Scabbards. The sexy Russian scientists stood alongside him, their belts poised over his buttocks.

Lin Saong said something in Chinese to Girl Number One and Girl Number Two. They promptly, and with eager smiles, shed their duds. Su Wing did likewise. I wrapped my arms around all three of the now-naked lovelies, and my fingers toyed with the breasts of Girls Number One and Two while my lips nibbled teasingly at Su Wing's neck.

It was Lin Saong's turn to undress.

She went about it slowly, bashfully.

And while bashfulness was never my cup of tea, I found

167

myself becoming incredibly aroused by her movements.

I recalled the evening of my first meeting with her at the hotel room in Port duBeers.

I remembered how, as she spoke to me, she had leaned forward in her chair.

Her bountiful, uncorseted breasts, unusually large for an Oriental girl, had jiggled invitingly against the contours of her loose-fitting blouse.

My well-trained eyes had made out the outlines of her firm, upthrust nipples, then had traversed the marvelous expanse of her sensuous slacks-encased thighs.

She had shifted in her seat, and her long legs had swung to one side. My eyes had zeroed in on the succulent curves of her hips, which had strained maddeningly against the tightness of her slacks.

Now these charms would be exposed completely to me.

A hot flame of desire took form in my stomach as she hoisted the hem of her sweater up toward her shoulders, and her uncorseted breasts popped out.

They were marvelous—round and firm and fully stacked. They stood proudly before her, their bullet-hard nipples alive with anticipation. I imagined my tongue tracing hot wet circles around them, and a shiver of excitement coursed through my body.

She tugged the sleeves of the sweater over her arms, and the magnificent mammaries danced wildly. Then she dropped the sweater in a heap on the floor.

My eyes feasted on the flawless beauty of her bare upper torso. It was a masterpiece of line and form, a creation which would have inspired any sculptor and which certainly was inspiring this lover.

Her fingers went to work on the buttons and zipper that held her slacks in place. My breath caught in my throat as she eased the slacks along the smooth expanse of her legs.

Her thighs were soft and shapely and unbelievably exciting. Her calves were full and round and gently curved. I felt my desire rise higher and higher.

Now the slacks were on the floor along with the sweater. She hooked her thumbs into the waistband of her panties and eased them over her exquisitely carved hips. Then,

168

with a subtle caressing motion, she lowered them to her ankles and delicately stepped out of them.

I felt myself tremble as she stood naked before me. She was a goddess, a Venus, a living poem to beauty. And she was mine—all mine.

"Do you like me?" she whispered hoarsely, as if no one else were in the room with us.

"I do," I whispered back. "Very, very much."

She smiled with a coquetry which belied her virgin state. "Then take me. But be gentle. Please be gentle."

My arms closed around her back, pressing her to me. My lips found hers, and my tongue entered her mouth. She sucked on it tenderly—first hesitantly, then with obvious relish.

My knee edged between her legs, and they parted. My fingers raked her back, then caressed the smooth, round mounds that were her buttocks. She shook with excitement, and her fingers tightly gripped my shoulders. Her Mount of Venus rubbed sensuously against my thigh.

I lowered her into place on the floor, and lay alongside her. My mouth covered one of her breasts, and my tongue licked teasingly at the nipple.

A minute passed, then another. Then she whispered, "Take me." Spreading her thighs, I gently launched my invasion.

Her body tensed as I entered it.

I eased back, and she relaxed.

Then I pressed forward with all the strength at my command. A startled gasp escaped from her throat as my hardness strained her endurance. Then the rampart yielded and I was immersed to the hilt.

She screamed.

Then she groaned.

Then her groans became moans, and her moans merged into sensuous sighs of pleasure.

Her body began squirming wildly beneath me. Her legs wrapped tightly around mine. Her fingers clawed at my back.

I motioned to Girl Number One and Girl Number Two, who hurried to my side. Clutching each by a leg, I maneuvered them into place on my flanks. They lay supine on the floor, their heads diagonal to my waist. Their tongues licked at my ribs and their breasts ground against my biceps as my hands cupped their Venus' Mounts and my fingers probed their Golden Crevices.

Now it was Su Wing's turn. I had her kneel over Lin Saong's face, then bend backwards until her shoulders were almost touching her ankles. The bright pink lips of her womanhood quivered excitedly as my mouth neared them.

Somewhere in the distance I could hear the sharp cracks of leather against flesh as Tania and Olga went to work on Douzi with their belts. The diminutive dictator's grunts echoed through the room. "Don't!" I heard him cry plaintively. Then, "Please! . . . oh, please! . . . oh, nooooo! ! !"

But I didn't pay much attention to him. I had too many other things on my mind.

Like Girl Number One and Girl Number Two. They were writhing fiercely in response to the stimulation of my fast-moving fingers. Their sweat-slick bodies rubbed against my arms, and their tongues lapped hungrily at my flesh.

And Su Wing. Her body was trembling like a reed as my tongue probed deeper and deeper into her hidden recesses.

And Lin Saong? She was enjoying the party more than anybody. Her legs were wrapped coil-tight around mine. Her fists were pummeling my back. Her teeth were biting fiercely into my neck.

My spine was tingling, and my pulse was pounding a mile a minute. I knew that it wouldn't be long before my volcano erupted.

And I'd have plenty of company when the eruption finally came. Su Wing's hips were hunching madly. Girl Number One and Girl Number Two were slithering like two snakes in a barrelful of slime. And Lin Saong was squirming to beat the band.

Off in the distance, I heard Tania say something in Russian to Olga. The cracking of leather against flesh abated, and Douzi's cries disintegrated into whimpers of relief. I had an idea what was happening—and that it was exactly what I'd been banking on. But I was too caught up in what

I was doing to bother to look up.

Su Wing's hip-movements had taken on an urgency which told me that release couldn't be more than a tongue-tip away. Girls Number One and Two were right out there on the edge of the ledge with her. And Lin Saong's frantic moans told me that her tremors had already started.

My muscles tensed. I knew that the explosion would come in seconds. My fingers and tongue began moving faster, so that my eager sexmates would get theirs when I got mine.

From the distance I heard footsteps. Then more footsteps. Some of them were light and dainty, like girls' footsteps should be. But others were emphatically masculine.

I wondered if, perchance, Douzi's committeemen had somehow or other managed to get free. But then I stopped wondering, because my attentions were captured completely by the shock waves of sensation that roared through me.

It was a blast and a half. Not one cell of my body escaped the soaring feeling that came up like thunder and convulsed me with its force. My head spun, my stomach churned, and my limbs shook like bamboo stalks in a high wind.

All four girls were right there with me. Su Wing's hips pressed against my face as if she were trying to drive my whole head up inside her. Girls Number One and Two bit and clawed at me like two panthers. Lin Saong shook as though she were in the advanced stages of St. Vitus's dance.

I waited until the last ember of sensation had flickered out. Then I slowly raised my head.

Tania was sitting on a chair in front of me. One of CHILLER's submachine guns was in her arms. Olga was sitting next to her. She had the other machine gun, and judging from the look in her eyes, she'd like nothing more than to use it on the CHILLER-chicks.

Su Wing's eyes swelled to the size of saucers. "I think, Madame Saong," she said quietly, "that we've been betrayed."

171

Lin Saong quickly flopped over on her stomach. For a long, silent moment she said nothing. Then tears welled up in her eyes, and she lowered her head. Balling her hands into fists, she began pounding on the floor.

"Sex!" she screamed. "Chairman Mao is right! It's so good—but it's so, so dangerous!"

"Not always," I observed softly. "Only when you don't know how to use it."

The girls from CHILLER climbed slowly to their feet. Tania gestured with her submachine gun, and Girls Number One and Two minced obediently toward the wall. She gestured again, and Su Wing followed them. Then she gestured a third time, and Lin Saong joined the group.

"Well, Damon," the CHILLER commander admitted grudgingly, "I guess you win."

"Yeah," I smirked.

"And," boomed a hearty bass voice behind me, "the Marines proved to be wholly unnecessary."

I wheeled around and saw who had been responsible for the masculine footsteps I'd heard earlier.

He was tall, gaunt and lean as a swizzle-stick. His weather-beaten face was a latticework of wrinkles, and the bags under his eyes were big enough to carry groceries home in.

Clinging to his arm was a statuesque brunette with jugs the size of softballs. Flanking the couple were two men, both mean-looking Cosa Nostra types with broken noses and cauliflower ears.

My eyes did a quick tour of the group, then returned to the face of its leader. He whistled a few bars of "From the Halls of Montezuma." Then he broke out in a warm smile and tugged playfully on the ends of his walrus-like moustache.

"Fancy meeting you here," I quipped.

"I was in the neighborhood," he replied, "and I just thought I'd drop in." He surveyed the room. His gaze rested momentarily on the Belgravian committeemen and the eunuch, who were still tied together in the middle of the floor. It rested a while longer on Douzi, whose tiny body remained draped over the chair on which he had been beaten.

172

It lingered appreciatively over the nude bodies of the four girls from CHILLER, who were huddled together against the wall as Olga covered them with her submachine gun. Then it fixed on lovely, long-legged Tania, who had come to my side and was cuddling me possessively. "Looks like you've been having quite the party. Sorry I didn't get here earlier."

"Oh well," I sighed philosophically, "better late than never."

His face lighted up as if he'd just heard the wittiest remark ever uttered. "Remind me to remind you to introduce me to your gag-writer. He must be a real winner."

My arm closed around Tania, pressing her to me. Her breasts felt just great against my bare chest. "Speaking of winners," I said, "let me introduce you to one of the finest collections of them ever assembled. First off, there's Dr. Douzi, who———"

"I know all about it," he cut me off. "We picked up on your radio broadcast tonight."

"I was hoping you would. In fact, I'd been hoping you would for five days now. What the hell took you so long?"

He shrugged. "When the radioman I sent to monitor you failed to report in, I sent another one. Lady Godiva here"—he nodded toward Lin Saong—"found out about him also and had him knocked off. That's when I decided I'd better look into the situation personally. So I flew to Belgravia with my boys, and———"

"And your girl," I put in, indicating the buxom brunette.

"All work and no play makes Jack horny. Anyway, we arrived in Port duBeers the day before yesterday, and thanks to your on-the-air loquaciousness, was picked up on you right away. When you started broadcasting tonight, we followed your beacon. Now here we are."

"Just in the nick of time, as they say in the movies."

"Actually we would have got here a lot sooner, but we had a flat tire. Sorry about that."

I remembered my quadruple coupling with the girls from CHILLER. "I'm not, now that I think of it." And I wasn't—not in the least bit.

He yawned elaborately. "Oh, well, so much for that. The

173

caper's over, and we've got new horizons to move on to."
He nodded to his two Cosa Nostra types. "Gentlemen,
would you be so kind as to round up all these people and
bring them out to the truck? Thank you. And you, Damon.
Would you be so kind as to put your clothes on and adjourn with me to my car? There's something I'd like to talk
to you about."

I suddenly had a funny feeling. And the feeling was
spelled t-r-o-u-b-l-e. "Oh no you don't," I said. "I've just
finished one caper, and a herd of wild horses couldn't drag
me into another one."

"Damon, Damon," he chuckled. "You're always so
suspicious, soooooo suspicious."

I held Tania to me. "It's not that I'm suspicious, pal. It's
just that I've found a chick I really dig, and I want to spend
some time with her. So whattaya say you give us both a
ride back to Port duBeers and drop us off at the handiest
hotel."

"I'd be delighted to. In fact, I'll even pay for your
room—and I'll buy your breakfast in the morning. We can
have our little chat then."

"I never turn down a free breakfast. But, I'm telling you
now: no more capers."

He smiled. "We'll talk about that when the morning
comes. Now let's be off, shall we? The hour grows late,
and"—he kissed the brunette playfully on the nose—"the
hotel rooms are waiting."

"We're off," I sighed, imitating his manner. "And may
the morning never come."